9339

Jessica

SPRINGSONG 🐾 BOOKS

Andrea   Kara

Anne   Kathy

Carrie   Leslie

Colleen   Lisa

Cynthia   Melissa

Erica   Michelle

Gillian   Paige

Jenny   Pamela

Jessica   Sara

Joanna   Sherri

Tiffany

Jessica

Melody Carlson

BETHANY HOUSE PUBLISHERS
MINNEAPOLIS, MINNESOTA 55438

Jessica
Melody Carlson

Library of Congress Catalog Card Number 96–25354.

ISBN 1–55661–861–1

Copyright © 1996

Cover design by Peter Glöege

Published by Bethany House Publishers
A Ministry of Bethany Fellowship, Inc.
11300 Hampshire Avenue South
Minneapolis, Minnesota 55438

Printed in the United States of America.

To Mom and Missy, with love.

MELODY CARLSON has published a number of short stories in various teen and children's magazines, as well as a child-care book and several picture books for children. A senior editor for Questar Publishers, Melody enjoys snow skiing, boating, and hiking with her husband and two teen-age sons.

1

*T*he room was dark and empty, except for a couple of guys Jessica vaguely recognized from school. The heady smell of fresh-ground coffee filled the air, and black-and-white checkerboard tiles covered the floor. A few large antiques and leafy plants occupied the corners, and many tiny tables congregated around a small stage, with a tall black stool in the center. Some unframed prints adorned the walls, and intriguing music drifted through the room, not like anything Jessica had heard before. It sounded like a cross between electronic and classical, peaceful and soothing.

"Welcome to the Blue Skye. Can I help you ladies?" asked a young man behind the counter.

Jessica admired his deep brown eyes with dark lashes. *Not bad—he must be new in town.*

"Uh, yes. I'd like some coffee," she stammered. Tawna giggled behind her. He flashed a bright smile and Jessica's heart beat a little faster.

"What kind would you like?" He glanced up at the menu board behind him. Jessica stared at the many different kinds: French Mocha, Cappuccino, Irish Cream, Almond Blend—so many to choose from. She had heard of cappuccino before, and it sounded sort of elegant.

"I'll have cappuccino," she announced with false confidence.

His eyebrows lifted. "Oh, so you're quite a coffee

drinker, I see." Was he making fun of her?

Jessica looked down and fumbled with her purse.

"I'll have what she's having," announced Tawna.

"Okay, two cappuccinos coming up." He turned and fiddled with a big shiny copper machine, then returned with two small steaming cups topped with white froth.

"Isn't he cute?" Tawna whispered as they sat down at a nearby table.

Jessica gave Tawna a sideways glance and sipped her cappuccino. She almost sputtered when the unexpected heat scorched her tongue.

"Isn't this a lovely place?" drawled Tawna in a fakey ultrasophisticated voice. Jessica rolled her eyes and wished for a glass of water.

"How's your cappuccino, Tawna?" Jessica asked, more for the waiter's sake.

Tawna took her first sip and made an awful face. "I can't drink this stuff, Jessica. It tastes like poison!"

"I know. Just pretend," whispered Jessica. She had just about had it with Tawna.

"Would you ladies care for some ice water?" the waiter asked with a great smile.

"Thanks," Jessica replied. She forced another sip and persuaded herself she could learn to appreciate cappuccino. Tawna wouldn't touch hers; instead she gulped down the ice water and told Jessica she wanted to leave.

"I hear Barry Bartowski plays guitar here," Jessica commented to the waiter as she and Tawna headed for the door. "Do you know when he performs?"

"Every night after seven or so, depending on the crowd. Do you like classical guitar?"

"Oh yes, I love it," exclaimed Jessica. She liked classical music and she liked guitar, so she reasoned she would probably like classical guitar.

"Then maybe I'll see you again," the waiter said with a sparkle in his eye.

The girls squinted in the afternoon sunlight after exiting the dimly lit coffeehouse. Jessica decided next time she would definitely come without Tawna. Something about the atmosphere in there was such a departure from the typical Midwestern way of life. And that waiter . . .

They decided to venture over to the mall. Tawna still had an hour to kill, and Greg wouldn't be ready until five. Jessica absently followed Tawna's well-worn path from shop to shop and endured her incessant chatter about new fashions, the latest CD, and how she never wanted to see another cup of cappuccino.

Finally at five, Jessica told Tawna goodbye and hurried over to Miller's Feed and Seed, where Greg worked. She was proud of her brother. He'd worked his way up to assistant manager. Everyone loved Greg Johnson—Poloma star quarterback and best bronc-buster in Kansas.

Jessica noticed the lights were off so she pushed on the door. It was locked. She glanced at her watch—only 5:03. Greg must have been in some kind of hurry! She should have told him she was in town and wanted to catch a ride. *Just great—now someone will have to make a special trip.* She walked over to Bailey's Market to use the phone but remembered the pay phone by the counter at the coffeehouse. It seemed a good excuse for a second glimpse of the Blue Skye, not to mention the waiter.

But he wasn't around. Instead an attractive slender girl with bleached-blond hair leaned against the counter. She wore all black and an expression that was a cross between boredom and arrogance.

"Can I help you?" she asked in what sounded like annoyance.

"No, I uh—I just came to use the pay phone," Jessica explained, lamely pointing to the phone on the wall.

"Fine, just use it then. That's what we're here for you know." She shook her head and abruptly turned away.

"Hi, Todd," Jessica said quietly into the receiver. She felt stupid and conspicuous. She should've used the phone at Bailey's. "I missed Greg—for my ride. And I need someone to get me. Sorry."

"Jess, Dad just got the swather running, and I need to get out there and finish up."

"I know, I'm sorry. How 'bout I hang out at the mall until someone can come? I'll get something to eat."

"Do you mind, Jess? I promise I'll be there by eight, okay?"

She hung up in frustration. Almost three hours to kill in a town about as lively as a sign post.

"Hi, there," said a vaguely familiar voice. "Sounds like a maiden in distress." She spun around to see the waiter leaning casually back against the counter, hands in his pockets as if he hadn't a care in the world.

"Oh, not too much distress. I just missed my ride home and have a few hours to kill. Nothing very serious." It surprised her how calmly she spoke, despite her flittering heart.

"Well, I'm heading out for a bite to eat. Want to join me? I guess I should introduce myself. I'm Barry Bar—"

"Bartowski!" she exclaimed. "You should have told us."

"Oh, I know. I just don't like to sound like I'm, you know . . . blowing my horn or something."

"Sure, I'd love to join you. I'm Jessica Johnson." She knew her parents had a policy—she could only date people they had met, but this wasn't really a date.

"Where you off to, Barry?" asked the blonde sweetly, nothing like the tone Jessica had heard earlier.

"Just out for a bite. Want me to bring you anything, Sara?"

"No, I've got some yogurt and a bagel in the fridge.

Don't be late for your show." She smiled at him and gave Jessica an icy look.

Main Street instantly took on a whole new appearance as she walked beside Barry toward the tiny mall. It no longer seemed so isolated and destitute. Even Hal's Diner gained an unexpected aura of romance.

"I'll have a cheeseburger basket and a Pepsi," Jessica announced without even glancing at the menu. The waitress licked her pencil and turned to Barry.

"I'll have your chef salad, but hold the meat. Do you have herbal tea?" The waitress shook her head with a smirky grin. "Mineral water?" he asked. She glared at him as if he were an alien. "Okay, how about just plain old-fashioned water?" The waitress laughed cynically and snapped her ticket book closed.

"I guess I shouldn't be so finicky, but I'm a vegetarian and it's difficult to find anything very palatable around this town."

"Really?" Jessica admired him. "It's obvious by your accent you're not from around here. I'm curious, how'd you come to be in Poloma, of all places?"

He chuckled. "You don't sound terribly thrilled with the Breadbasket of America."

"Well, sometimes I just crave something more . . . you know . . ." She stared off dreamily. "Sometimes I dream of living in places like Paris or maybe New York. Even Wichita sounds more interesting than here." She couldn't believe she had divulged one of her secrets to a perfect stranger. But then Barry didn't seem like a stranger.

"I know what you mean, Jessica. I used to feel that way, but after I lived abroad for a while, I learned to appreciate this country and its possibilities. But I have to admit our culture could use some refinement, especially in places like—no offense, but Poloma."

She nodded and watched him in amazement. Was this

all a dream? But the smell of her broiled burger brought her back to reality, and she noticed Barry already poking around his salad.

"Aren't you going to eat?" he asked with one of those smiles. Jessica laughed and picked up her cheeseburger. It looked kind of mundane now, but after a hard day's work she knew she should be starving.

"Where are you from, Barry?"

"All over. I guess you could call me a citizen of the world."

"Really? You don't look old enough to have been too many places." It was a bold hint, but she was curious.

"Well, I started life early. I've been on my own since I was sixteen. I went to college in New York for a while, but it was such a narrow environment, I decided to let the world educate me instead. And I'm not ashamed to admit I'm only twenty. How old are you, Jessica?"

Suddenly sixteen sounded very young, but honesty had always been her way. "Sixteen," she replied. His eyes widened. "Well, actually, sixteen and a half."

"Only sixteen? And I was sure you were out of high school. You seem very grown up for your age."

She smiled and dipped a fry in ketchup. "You never told me how you came to be in Poloma."

"Oh, that's simple. A friend from New York, Arnie Baker, started this coffeehouse. He invited me to come and provide entertainment to help get it going. That's his daughter Sara you saw at the counter. She can be kind of witchy sometimes, but once you get to know her she's not so bad. Anyway, I'm not sure how long I'll stick around. Sometimes I feel pretty cramped in this little cow town."

"That's too bad, but I guess I understand." She frowned. Lately she had felt cramped too, and the feeling confused her. She loved her family and even the land, but sometimes she felt so confined by the Kansas wide-open spaces.

"But people like you give me hope," he continued. "At least a few Poloma citizens appreciate a broader view of life—something beyond rodeos and T-bone steaks. And I sense you're one of them, Jessica." He glanced at his watch. "Speaking of which, I better get back and warm up my guitar. Can you come or will your ride be here?"

"Well, I don't have to meet Todd until eight. That gives me more than an hour. Sure, I'll come."

"Todd? Is that your boyfriend?"

Jessica grinned. "No—my brother—one of three. They're all older. I'm the baby." *What a stupid thing to say*, she thought with regret.

"Well, you can't blame me for assuming a girl as pretty as you might have a boyfriend or two strung along."

"Well, currently I'm footloose and fancy-free," she announced happily. He laughed and paid their bill.

"Hey, I didn't expect you to buy my dinner."

"Sorry, I didn't mean to offend you. Maybe next time you'll buy mine."

She liked the insinuation and hoped she'd get the chance.

———

Jessica watched Barry in fascination. His guitar music captivated her, and she discovered she really did like classical guitar. In between numbers he read in a deep, resonant voice—almost hypnotic. First a utopic poem on world peace. Another reading raged against the narrow conformities of Western religion. She questioned it a little, but it sounded plausible. Just when he began an essay on meditation, she was forced to leave because it was eight o'clock.

———

"Hey, there you are, Jess!" Todd yelled from the other end of the mall. "I've been looking all over. Where've you been?"

"Just around," she answered quietly, not wishing to break the mystical spell Barry had woven over her.

Jessica watched the sunset with reverence as they rode home in silence. The clear Kansas sky had become a painter's canvas with wide strokes of periwinkle blue and a few touches of pink stretched across the horizon. She knew Barry would appreciate its beauty. . . .

2

*J*essica stood before her dresser and tried to see herself as Barry might. Her dimly lit dormer room didn't make it easy. A century-old farmhouse, though interesting, had its drawbacks. She wiped the dust from the surface of her mirror and took a quick inventory. Straight nose, heart-shaped face, gray-blue eyes, and long, curly, dark brown hair.

She considered Sara Baker from the coffeehouse, mentally comparing Sara's flawless appearance to her own. Sara had such a sophisticated, New Yorkish look, plus an interesting sort of frailty with her pale, almost translucent skin. Jessica, in contrast, was tall and strong with a golden tan. Why did she have to have such healthy farmgirl looks? She would probably make a good model for a dairy maid commercial, posing right next to a big Guernsey. She attempted a different expression by lifting her brows slightly and jutting her chin out in an air of indifference, similar to Sara.

"Jessica," her mother called. "Greg said to tell you he got that new video you've been wanting to see, and he's starting it now."

"In a minute, Mom." Jessica stuck her tongue out at her reflection and flipped off the light.

Downstairs, her mind refused to focus on the movie. Instead she discreetly scrutinized her family while they relaxed around the living room. Dad was already asleep in his recliner, his mouth gaping open and a toe protruding from a hole in his dirty sock. Jessica's oldest brother, Danny Jr., slumped back into the worn plaid couch. His wife, April, by his side, was crocheting a yellow baby afghan spread across her bulging mid-section—it was the first Johnson grandbaby and Mom was thrilled. Greg, who'd just gotten home, munched noisily on a leftover pork chop, and Todd sprawled across the thread-bare braided rug, watching the movie with eyes half-mast. There they were, the Johnson family in all their glory. Jessica knew they were tired after a long, hard day, but they really did look like a bunch of hicks.

With guilt, she heard Mom still in the kitchen getting things laid out for breakfast. Mornings came early this time of year. It used to be Jessica's job to help Mom, but when Danny Jr. married April last year they decided to live on the farm, and April took over Jessica's chores. Jessica was glad to work outside, and Dad appreciated an extra farmhand.

Jessica wondered how Barry might view her family. Why did she keep thinking of him? He'd probably laugh at them and their corny ways. Nothing but a bunch of meat-eating bumpkins! At her feet lay Betsy, their old border collie, nearly blind now and exuding an aroma only her dearest friends could endure. Jessica patted Betsy and shook her head in dismay. The movie turned out to be a disappointment, and Jessica slipped back to her room.

She retrieved an old diary from the bottom of her sock drawer and looked inside. It had been a gift from Todd, but she hadn't written in it since she was thirteen, and then only a few pages. But she felt compelled to write now. Maybe it was the earnest depth of Barry's readings, or maybe it was just Barry, but she wrote and wrote until she filled up six pages. This time she locked the tiny book and hid the key.

––––––––––

The next day was Saturday, and Jessica worked hard to get chores done by early afternoon. She had promised Zephyr a ride, but now she wondered if that was such a good idea. It felt like it was one hundred degrees out. Zephyr approached her with friendly eagerness, and Jessica rewarded him with a big, dirty carrot fresh from the garden and a nuzzle on the nose. His nose was soft and smelled sweet from alfalfa hay. She kicked her boots off and climbed onto his broad, dusty back.

"Still want to go out in this heat, old boy?" Jessica asked, stroking his faded gray mane. Zephyr was all hers. Dad had brought him home when she was eight. Zephyr had been exactly the same age and as dependable as the Kansas blue sky. Dad had offered to trade him for a younger horse, but she couldn't accept. Zephyr was more than a horse; he was her confidante and friend. He understood Jessica and knew all her secrets. As he plodded toward the irrigation pond, she told him another.

"I met a handsome prince yesterday, Zephyr. His eyes are like deep, dark pools. I think I could swim in them. His name is Barry and he's not like anyone I've ever known. He's intelligent and sensitive. I think I might be in love. . . ."

When they reached the pond, she let Zephyr walk right in. The cold water rushed up her bare legs with tingling freshness. A clump of cottonwoods whispered softly in the slight breeze, and all around her stretched endless fields in varying shades of green for as far as she could see.

"Yep, old Zeph, someday I'll leave this place, and I'll find what's out there. I'll travel the world, see castles and kings. But I'll come back, don't you worry. I'll never forget my old Zephyr boy." Jessica wrapped her arms around Zephyr's neck and slid into the cool wetness. She sunk down into the pond, allowing the water to stun the top of her sun-baked head with its icy coldness. She held her breath until the pulse throbbed loudly in her ears and her lungs begged for air. Springing up, she shook her wet curls and watched the droplets fly like glittering diamonds in sunlight.

In the distance, she heard Mom calling her name. She

quickly climbed back onto Zephyr, creating a slick, muddy puddle on his back. Hanging on tight she galloped him over to the back porch.

"What's wrong?" she yelled.

Mom waved from the steps, her face flushed. "It's April, honey," Mom began, wringing a dish towel in her hands. "She's not feeling so good. I think she needs to go to town and see Doc Martin. It's probably nothing, but the guys are all out on the west side haying, and I thought maybe you could take her in. I need to get supper on."

"Sure, Mom, just let me put Zephyr up and I'll be right back. Tell April to be ready."

———

April sat silently in Todd's old pickup while Jessica navigated the multitude of potholes in the long driveway. April's face was pasty, and she clutched the edge of the seat with white knuckles.

"You okay, April?" Jessica asked with concern. She'd never thought much of April one way or another. She had always seemed kind of whiny to Jessica. But now she felt a pang of sympathy for her sister-in-law. It might be scary being pregnant, and on top of that, April's family had sold their farm and moved off to Florida last fall.

"I think I'm all right, but I don't know. . . ." She began to cry. "If only Danny could come—"

"Don't worry, April. I'm sure everything's fine. It's probably just this heat getting to you. I wish this pickup had air conditioning." All the same Jessica speeded up. It was still a month before April's due date, but Jessica didn't want to deliver a baby on the road. It probably wouldn't be anything like calving.

———

It was cool inside Dr. Martin's office, and soon April

calmed down and even browsed through a baby magazine while they waited.

"April Johnson," the receptionist called. Jessica looked at April inquisitively, willing but not eager to go in.

"It's okay, Jessie. Why don't you go get yourself a pop or something?"

With a sigh of relief Jessica left the stuffy doctor's office and headed toward Main Street. Today there was more activity in town. Saturdays were like that. She glanced at her watch and walked straight toward the coffeehouse—she'd allow herself twenty minutes for another possible glimpse of Barry.

The familiarity at the Blue Skye welcomed her—its smells, sounds, and atmosphere. It was busier today. She spotted Shelly Henderson across the room with a girl she had never seen before. There at the counter stood Barry wearing a loose, white collarless shirt, smiling, looking cool and cosmopolitan. At once Jessica grew uncomfortably aware of her own grungy appearance and realized that just forty minutes earlier she'd been sitting on the bottom of a muddy irrigation pond. Although the heat had dried her clothes, she must look disgusting. Ready to bolt, she noticed Barry smiling her way. Hesitantly she approached the counter, wishing, not for the first time, that she wasn't such an impulsive person. Why hadn't she thought this through?

"What'll you have, Jessica?" He leaned forward and looked straight into her eyes.

"Oh, I don't know." She glanced at the menu board and stifled the desire to smooth her wind-blown hair. Sara was operating the coffee machine. She looked so sleek and smooth in a sleeveless black dress, her pale blond hair gleaming under the lights.

"Well," Barry began in a lowered voice. "You're not really much of a coffee drinker are you, Jessica?" She looked up in surprise. "It's okay," he continued. "We all start somewhere. Now how about a nice cup of French Mocha?" She nodded and he quickly returned with a creamy-looking coffee, a glass of ice water, and a little piece of what looked like dried-up toast, all neatly arranged on a tray.

"And what's this?" she asked, indicating the funny lump of bread but not wanting to sound too uncultured.

"It's called biscotti, a Jewish pastry of sorts. It's excellent with coffee. My treat," he winked. "Are you coming again tonight?"

"Oh, I don't know. Maybe," she answered hopefully.

"Hey, Jessie," called a female voice. "Over here." Jessica saw Shelly wave. Now this was a surprise. Shelly Henderson didn't usually give Jessica the time of day. Shelly was the girl who had it all—brains, style, boyfriends, and money. . . .

"Oh hi, Shelly, how are you doing?"

"Great. Join us?" Shelly pulled out a chair. "I didn't know you came here, Jessie. Doesn't this place just brim with atmosphere? A lot of my friends don't appreciate it, but it's nice to find someone who does. By the way, Jessie, this is Danielle Jones, my cousin from Connecticut. She's been visiting the last two weeks. In fact, she's the one who got me hooked on this place." Jessica didn't quite know what to think of all this unexpected friendliness.

"It reminds me of a spot at home. Besides, I thought old Shel' could use a little refinement," laughed Danielle. Then in a conspiratorial tone she said, "We noticed you're on a first-name basis with Mr. Bartowski. Isn't he cute? Shelly's been flirting with him all week." Danielle nudged Shelly with her elbow.

Now Jessica understood. Well, they could think what they liked about her and Barry. She didn't mind.

"I haven't flirted, Danielle. You know I already have a boyfriend, even if he is working at a camp all summer! I just happen to find Barry extremely interesting. Not only that, I enjoy his music and reading. It helps to expand my little uncultured mind." Shelly jabbed Danielle back.

"I just discovered this place too," said Jessica. "I really like it. It's just what Poloma needs to evolve from the dark ages." The girls laughed.

"I'm surprised, Jessie," said Shelly. "I'd always thought of you as—well, you know—sort of the typical cowgirl type. This is a new side to you."

Jessica finished her last sip and noticed the time. "Uh-oh, gotta go. I left my sister-in-law at the doctor."

"You coming tonight?" asked Shelly. "We could swing by your place and give you a ride."

Jessica couldn't believe her luck. "Sure, that'd be great."

"Around eight?"

Jessica agreed and headed for the door. She checked the counter for Barry, but he wasn't around. She dashed back to the doctor's, trying to concoct a good excuse for being late.

"About time," exclaimed April, closing a magazine.

"Sorry, April, I saw some friends. And you know how time flies. . . ."

"Yeah sure, I vaguely remember those days," April said with sarcasm. She patted her swollen middle with a frown. "Well, the baby's fine. You were probably right about the heat. Doc Martin said I should take it easier though."

———

Supper was on the table when they got back. Fortunately Mom had said nothing about April, so no one was concerned. Mom was forever the peace-keeper of the family. They bowed their heads as usual, and Dad prayed his standard supper-time grace. But Jessica's mind was fifteen miles down the main road, with a handsome young man and a little coffeehouse.

Her family joked and teased across the table. It was their usual summer fare, chilled smoked ham, potato salad, and all sorts of homemade things. Jessica wondered how her mother could stand it day after day. But Mom didn't seem to weary of the never-ending food preparations, and she rarely complained. Though today she looked more worn than usual, her faded brown hair tinged with gray and her sad flowered dress hanging limp and lifeless.

After supper, the guys returned to haying and Jessica offered to clean the kitchen, sending Mom and April out to the porch swing. In all honesty her helpfulness was dual-purposed. She wanted to give Mom a break, but even more so she wanted no friction about going to the Blue Skye for the evening. She finished in record time and dashed upstairs for a quick, cool shower. She vigorously scrubbed her hair and scolded herself for letting Barry see her looking like such a derelict today. She probably had pond slime dripping from her hair.

She rummaged through her closet again and again, from one end to the next, as if something new and interesting might be lurking back there. Finally, she pulled on a soft pink rayon sundress. Quaint, perhaps, but that was her style. She looked critically at her reflection in the mirror and added a touch of pink lipstick. It was already after eight, and she hurried downstairs to find Mom in the kitchen.

"Oh, Jessica, you're pretty as a picture," exclaimed Mom, giving her a warm squeeze. "Thanks for your help in the kitchen. What are you up to—date tonight?"

"Nah, just going with Shelly Henderson to the coffee-house—"

"You gotta be kidding!" Greg exclaimed from the back porch. He dumped dust from his cowboy boots on the steps. "That's a pretty weird place if you ask me, Jessie. You don't want to hook up with that crowd. Bunch of kooks from what I hear."

Jessica frowned at Greg. "Well, I don't think you really know what you're talking about, Greg, and besides, I didn't ask you." It wasn't easy being the little sister, but over the years Jessica had learned how to hold her own with her sometimes bossy brothers. "And for your information, I happen to find the Blue Skye intellectually stimulating." Just then a horn blared in the drive. "See ya later. Don't wait up, Mom!"

———

The coffeehouse was nearly crowded tonight. Jessica noticed once again the kids from school she might have considered losers at one time. Seeing them here improved her opinion of them. She sat with Shelly and Danielle. After two cups of French Mocha, Barry still hadn't noticed her. But every fibre of her being honed onto him like radar as he read a philosophical essay on multiculturalism. Then she closed her eyes and became lost in his music. During his breaks she tried not to stare but occasionally glimpsed in his direction.

"Looks like Sara's putting the move on Barry tonight," whispered Shelly. Jessica peeked out of the corner of her eye and spied Sara rubbing Barry's back affectionately. Jessica's insides twisted with what she knew must be jealousy. But what was she to him anyway? Just a mere acquaintance.

The next poem he read was about the price of love and seemed focused in Sara's direction. Yet it sliced through Jessica's heart like a cold steel blade. From the corner of her eye, she watched Sara leaning nonchalantly against the counter. She was refined and self-assured, sipping a tiny cup of espresso, a faint smile playing across her lips. Jessica glanced down at her own silly pink dress. She looked like she was ready for the annual Sunday school picnic. She was so unsophisticated. Why should Barry look twice at her? After her third cup of French Mocha, she noticed Barry's arm draped around Sara's shoulders. He threw his head back and laughed as if Sara were the most amusing thing in Kansas.

Finally, Shelly was ready to leave. Jessica stood in relief mixed with disappointment. When they reached the door, Barry left Sara and approached Jessica.

"Jessica, I didn't know you were here tonight." He touched her arm. His hand on her bare skin burned like fire, and her head seemed to swim. "You leaving so soon?"

She nodded dumbly.

His hand was still on her arm. "And you look so pretty too. Just like the farmer's daughter." She smiled stiffly and mumbled goodbye.

All the way home, Jessica fumed in the back of Shelly's Blazer. Just what did he mean by "farmer's daughter"?

"Well, Jessie," Shelly said. "Looks like Barry still remembers your name. But did you get a load of him and snooty Sara?"

Danielle laughed. "Let Sara have him—right Jessie? I think they both have a superiority complex anyway!"

Jessica forced a laugh. Still she resented the remark about Barry, and the fact that she resented it made her even more mad.

———

The next day on their way to church, Jessica, as always, rode with Todd. He was just a year older, and they'd always understood each other. Sometimes it was almost like they could read each other's minds, and unlike most siblings, they rarely fought. Jessica wondered what Todd thought of the coffeehouse, but she didn't care to bring it up. He was quieter than usual as he drove down the highway, and it suited her just fine.

Finally, he broke the silence. "I hear you've been going to the coffeehouse."

She nodded, unwilling to discuss this subject with even

her favorite brother. She blankly watched wheat fields roll by, some full and uncut and those from winter wheat already reduced to stubble and chaff.

Todd cleared his throat. "Jess, you think it's a good idea to hang out there? I mean, I've heard there might even be some drug dealing with that crowd—"

"You know, Todd, I get so tired of this Midwest mentality, 'if something's different it's gotta be bad.' Everybody's so judgmental around here. I'm surprised at you, though, Todd. I always thought you had an open mind. But there you go judging, and I'll bet you've never even been inside!"

"Well, no, but I've heard stuff. I can't explain it, Jess. I just get this funny feeling every time I walk by there—"

"A 'funny feeling'! Come on Todd, grow up! You're almost eighteen, and sometimes you act so immature!"

Todd's jaw grew firm, and he drove on in stony silence. Why was she snapping his head off? "Todd, I'm sorry. It's just that sometimes I get so hungry for something different. I don't know why, but I like the Blue Skye. Maybe you'd like it too. You should go sometime and see for yourself."

Todd's brow creased. "Well, Jess, maybe I will. . . ."

———

In church, Jessica imagined what Barry might think of their old-time religion. Probably laugh his head off. Just like he did with Sara last night. He was probably laughing at Jessica then, in her little pink dress looking just like the 'farmer's daughter.'

3

*T*he next few days Jessica pushed thoughts of Barry far into the recesses of her mind. She immersed herself in chores and farm activities. Even so, something restless stirred within her. Everyday things no longer interested her, and she couldn't imagine a life more boring than her own.

Later in the week Shelly called to invite Jessica to the Blue Skye, and she eagerly accepted. Shelly's cousin had gone back to Connecticut, and now Jessica looked forward to getting better acquainted with Shelly.

"Jessie?" asked Danny, knocking the dust from his cap. "You're not going to the Slacker Cafe tonight—are you?"

"Huh? What do you mean?" She squinted up at him from the porch swing. He was her oldest brother and looked more like Dad each day; same reddish hair and ruddy complexion. And now even his face bore a paternal frown. Jessica looked down and buckled her sandal, hoping Shelly would come soon and rescue her from this inquisition.

"You know what I mean, Jessie," he continued without budging from the porch. "Those kids that hang out there are just a bunch of losers. You don't fit in, Jessie. You're not like them." Shelly's bright red Blazer zipped up the driveway, enveloped in a cloud of dust.

"Sorry, Danny Boy, no time to chat." She darted off, thankful to have avoided another conflict. Her family seemed to be getting narrower and more uninformed all the time.

"Shelly Henderson!" exclaimed Jessica as she hopped

into the Blazer. "What have you done to your hair?" Shelly's previously shoulder-length auburn hair was now cropped short and dyed jet black.

"Isn't it cool?" gushed Shelly. "I feel like a new person. My parents had this absolute fit! It was great! For once, I felt totally free of inhibition. It's so great, Jessica. I don't even care if anyone likes it or not, you know what I mean?"

"I think so." Jessica wasn't so sure and tried not to stare at Shelly's hair.

At the Blue Skye, Barry only spoke to Jessica once. Most of his spare moments seemed to be occupied with Sara. Finally he approached their table, but unfortunately Sara was right on his heels. Shelly invited them both to sit down.

"Shelly," exclaimed Sara. "Love the new look. You've made such a statement with your hair." Jessica watched Shelly's face. She was obviously flattered, yet appeared nonchalant.

"Thanks," Shelly remarked casually. "I needed to exert my individuality, you know. Get in touch with the inner me."

"Cool," Barry said with an approving smile. Suddenly Jessica felt alienated. She was the odd person out. Her hair, her clothes, everything about her didn't fit here. It was just like Danny had said.

Barry placed a hand on her shoulder. "Coming tomorrow night, Jessica? We're having a dance to celebrate the Blue Skye's one-month anniversary in Poloma. Quite a milestone." He laughed cynically. "But I hope you'll be here." He looked straight into her eyes and suddenly she could hardly breathe. His hand felt charged with electricity as the current flowed through her shoulder and down her arm.

On their way home, Shelly chattered away a mile a minute. Jessica tried to listen, but her own muddled feelings made it difficult to concentrate. Just when she'd given up all hope on Barry, he'd noticed her again.

"Earth to Jessie," Shelly said for the third time, interrupting Jessica's thoughts. "Are you still with me, or did martians invade your body and take over your brain?"

"Sorry, Shelly. What were you saying?"

"I said, I'm driving over to Crandell tomorrow to do some shopping. They have this really cool shop on campus. Their clothes are unique. Nothing like you'd find in Poloma. Want to come with me?"

"I'd love to, Shelly." Jessica knew she shouldn't accept without checking at home. This was their busy time of year. But why shouldn't she be able to spend a day with a friend once in a while? "How 'bout I call you in the morning?"

"Okay, just not before eight. I need my beauty sleep, you know." Shelly laughed. Jessica wondered if Shelly ever helped with chores. Shelly's dad was a farmer too, but with their huge spread they used hired hands.

———————

The porch light still burned, but the house was dark inside. Jessica heard soft footsteps in the kitchen and peeked in to see Mom standing by the window in her worn chenille bathrobe.

"You're not waiting up for me are you?" asked Jessica.

"No, not really," Mom said as she reached for a glass. "I just wanted some milk to help me sleep."

Jessica didn't quite believe her but decided to seize the opportunity. "Well, I'm glad you're up, because I wanted to ask you something."

Mom's face lit up. "Would you like some milk, Jessica?"

"Sure." She sat at the formica-topped kitchen table. Milk sounded good. She found she had a hard time falling asleep on nights after visiting the Blue Skye. She could never tell if it was Barry or just the caffeine. She watched Mom pour milk into a tall blue glass.

"I wondered if you'd mind if I went to Crandell with Shelly Henderson—to do some shopping tomorrow?"

"I think that'd be fine, Jessica. It sounds like things are pretty caught up around here. Dad was just saying what a difference it's made having you outside taking care of the stock this year. He said you work as hard as the boys." Jessica smiled, and Mom continued. "And April's feeling a lot better. Are you doing some back-to-school shopping? I guess it doesn't hurt to start early."

"Yeah, Shelly knows where some good shops are." Jessica picked at the loose corner of formica on the table. She couldn't think of anything else to say.

"Is that all you wanted to talk about, Jessica?" Mom stared into her empty milk glass, almost as if she had something to say.

"Uh-huh. I'll do my morning chores before I go." Jessica swigged the last of her milk and got up to rinse her glass.

"Well, honey," Mom began. She had that tone in her voice that made Jessica not want to listen. "I think you should know, your Dad and I are a little concerned about all the time you're spending at this Blue Skye place. We're not sure it's such a good thing. . . ."

Jessica stared down at the stained porcelain sink with clenched teeth. She'd wondered when Mom would put her two cents in. Everyone else had.

"Mom, I'm sixteen and a half. Don't you think I'm old enough to choose my own friends?" Mom didn't answer, and Jessica went on in exasperation. "Why can't you just trust me to handle my own life? I haven't blown it so far, have I?"

Mom sighed and shook her head. "We're just concerned—"

"I'm going to bed," Jessica interrupted. "Good night, Mother!"

———

The next day Jessica got up earlier than usual. She jumped right into her chores and was nearly finished by eight-thirty.

She called Shelly from the shop to confirm their trip.

"Hi, Jess," said Todd. "Sounds like you could use a hand if you're leaving by ten. Want some help with the hogs?"

"Sure. You know it's my favorite job. I don't see why Dad ever decided to keep pigs. I hope he doesn't do it again next year, because I for one am sick of Eau de la Hog."

Todd laughed as they carried the heavy slop buckets to the pen. "Hey, Jess, remember you wanted me to come to the Blue Skye sometime. How 'bout tonight?"

"Oh—umm, I don't know about tonight, Todd. . . . How about later on this week?"

"You mean you're not going tonight?"

"Probably not." Jessica tasted the lie. It was thick and dry and made it hard to talk. But she just didn't want Todd there—not tonight. "You know, Shelly and I might not get back from Crandell till late." Todd nodded and dumped her bucket for her.

———————

All the way to Crandell, Shelly and Jessica talked nonstop. Lately she had begun to feel closer to Shelly. It was like they were on the same wavelength, and the two-hour trip flew by.

"The best shop is called 'Age Nova.' It's really cool," Shelly said as they walked through the University district. "It's right next to that secondhand store." The shop was situated with several others in an old brick building.

"Look, it's got the same floor as the Blue Skye," Jessica pointed out, noticing the big black-and-white tiles.

"Sign of good taste." Shelly laughed as she rifled through the racks. "Hey, look at this." She held up a simple black dress, similar to the one Sara had worn. "This'd be cute on you, Jessie."

Jessica held it up in front of a cloudy antique mirror. "Cool, I'll try it." Before long, she found a few other pieces, all similar to styles she'd seen on Sara. The prices were a bit staggering, but Jessica figured it'd be worth it, especially if it helped win Barry's attention and approval. Besides, it was her own money that she'd saved up for school clothes. She and Shelly would be the trendsetters at Poloma High next fall. They both tried on all sorts of things. Every time Jessica saw Shelly in an outfit, it looked just perfect. But Jessica felt awkward and ridiculous in everything she tried.

"Be honest, Shelly. This just doesn't look right, does it?" Jessica asked as she stepped out in the sleeveless black dress.

"I don't know. . . ." Shelly frowned. "The dress fits real good. But something's not quite right. . . . Maybe it's your hair? I think it's all wrong for these styles. I mean, your hair's pretty, Jessie, but it's just so, so—"

"Old-fashioned!" Jessica finished Shelly's sentence. The store clerk stood nearby, surveying them without saying anything.

"What do you think?" Jessica inquired of the clerk. She was tall and thin and also wore clothes that looked like they were from this shop. Her hair was cut similar to Shelly's.

"Well, the dress is superb, but your friend's right. The hair's gotta go." She straightened a rack of leather jackets and turned around to look at Jessica. "There's a fantastic hair salon just two doors down. It's where I get mine done. . . ."

"Okay, I'll take these," Jessica announced, thrusting a handful of garments at the clerk. "And this dress too. Then we'll check out that hair place."

The busy hair shop had one opening for later that afternoon.

"That gives us time for lunch," said Shelly. "And there's a great restaurant just a few blocks over. I went there with my mom once. Of course, my mom hated it." They entered another old brick building, actually a renovated warehouse.

"Hey, this place is cool. Kind of reminds me of the Blue Skye too," said Jessica as they were seated.

"Yeah, pretty cool," Shelly agreed. She browsed the

menu. "I guess I'll have the spinach salad. It's really delicious. Oh, by the way, this is a vegetarian restaurant. But they have veggie-burgers." Jessica ordered the same as Shelly and quickly devoured the salad.

As they left the restaurant, Jessica still felt hungry. She'd skipped breakfast, and her chores had left her with a hefty appetite. But she soon forgot her hunger as they browsed through interesting shops and picked up a few accessories to go with their new look.

"Jessie, we'll be the hottest thing at Poloma High this fall," Shelly said. "Hey, it's almost time for your appointment. We better drift. I can't wait to see what they do with your hair."

The receptionist at the hair shop had a gold hoop and a diamond pierced through her right nostril. Jessica couldn't count how many earrings pierced her ears. Everyone in the shop wore similar hairstyles, so Jessica had no problem describing what she wanted.

She sat in the chair and stared at her reflection in the mirror, suddenly unsure. What would her family think? Well, it was her hair, and her life. Let them think what they want! The scissors snipped steadily, but Jessica decided not to look in the mirror. Instead she watched the thick brown curls fall limply to the floor.

"With your curly hair, you'll need lots of styling gel to get the right look," said the stylist. "Unless you chemically treat it, of course." The woman spun her chair around to face the mirror, and Jessica looked up. She felt sick. Her freshly cut hair was curlier than ever. She looked like a brunette Shirley Temple. Nothing like the sleek style she'd envisioned.

"Oh no! It's all wrong," Jessica exclaimed, holding back tears. Her long hair was better than this!

Just then Shelly wandered in from the waiting area and burst into giggles. "Oh, Jessie, you look like my mom's poodle, Cocoa Puff."

Jessica grew desperate. "Do something!" she pleaded to

the hairdresser who looked on with indifference. "This will never work! What did you mean when you said 'chemically treated'?"

"Oh, you know, straightening, bleaching, whatever—"

"That's it, Jessie!" Shelly exclaimed. "Bleach it! You'd look terrific as a blonde!"

At this point Jessica wished she could turn back the clock, go home, and forget this whole stupid thing. But already in this deep, she'd have to see it through. "Okay, go ahead—bleach it," she announced flatly. "But I don't want to see it until you're finished."

The stylist looked at her watch and frowned. "I guess I have time." After what felt like hours of having her hair pulled, drenched, dried, and styled, she gazed into the mirror with trepidation.

"It's perfect!" Shelly exclaimed from behind. Jessica couldn't believe her eyes. It looked almost like Sara's. Though shocking to see, she liked it. She looked older, and it even gave her a feeling of power, as though she was in control of her life. She no longer looked like the farmer's daughter. And she didn't care what her family said.

"Jessie, it's after five." Shelly was getting impatient. "Now we'll barely make it home and have time to get ready to go to the Blue Skye."

"Maybe we could change here," Jessica suggested. She imagined the reception her new look would receive at home. Besides, she'd told Todd she wasn't going to the coffeehouse tonight. "Then we could take our time and get some dinner—my treat."

Shelly agreed and the stylist let them change in the back room.

"Very elegant, ladies," the owner of the shop complimented them as he counted out the till. "You look ready for a hot night on the town." They laughed and thanked him.

Jessica felt so grown up as they paraded through the University district.

"It might be fun to go to college here," Jessica remarked.

"Not me," exclaimed Shelly. "This is strictly small potatoes. I plan to go back East to school. I, for one, am tired of cowboy country."

———

The Blue Skye looked busy as they pulled into the parking lot. Shelly parked in back. Some guys huddled together in the back alley, smoking what didn't smell like ordinary cigarettes. They whistled and hooted, but the girls pretended to ignore them as they slipped past and in the back door.

Once inside, Jessica and Shelly joined some friends. They were kids Jessica had known all her life, but they didn't even recognize her at first. She loved it! It was like becoming a whole new person—no longer the Johnson boys' kid sister.

The Blue Skye was definitely catching on. The dance hadn't begun yet, and Jessica listened intently to Barry's last reading. Tonight Jessica drank espresso and actually enjoyed the strong, bitter taste. *This is so cool,* she thought. *Our own little piece of culture, right here in Poloma.* She and Shelly were on the cutting edge; they even fit in with Sara and Barry. Electronic music started to play, and a few couples danced.

Barry approached their table, and Jessica could hardly suppress her excitement, dying to see his reaction to this new look. "Hi there, Shelly," he began. "Where's Jessica tonight?" Unable to control it any longer, she burst into laughter. He looked down at her in surprise, then broke into one of the best smiles she'd ever seen.

"Jessica Johnson! I can't believe it's you!" He reached for her hands and pulled her to her feet, taking a long, hard look. Jessica's cheeks burned with embarrassment, then pleasure. "Is it really you?" he whispered. "You look fantastic, Jessica—incredible. Let's dance."

She felt like Cinderella, transformed and dancing with the prince at the ball. But like Cinderella, she had her limitations. She phoned home after a while to let them know she'd be getting in late. Barry came with two espressos and led her to an empty table. She noticed Sara scowl darkly behind the counter.

"Jessica, you've changed so much this past week," said Barry, taking her hands in his. "You totally fascinate me. You're like this beautiful butterfly—metamorphosing, emerging, and evolving into a lovely, worldly creature." She listened to his hypnotic prose, losing herself in his dark eyes. They danced again, and when he held her close it nearly took her breath away. She'd had some brief romances before, but never anything like this.

"Jessie," Shelly interrupted between dances. "I'm beat, and it's after midnight. I want to go home—are you coming?"

"Stay a little longer, Jessica," Barry whispered. "I'll take you home." Jessica knew she should go. But he stroked her bare arm with his fingertips, and she couldn't make herself leave.

"Go ahead without me, Shelly."

They danced some more. The songs were all slow now, and he held her tight. Jessica wondered if she might just melt in his arms. She'd never felt like this before.

"I know I haven't known you that long, Jessica, but I know this—I love you," Barry whispered in her ear.

Tingles ran down her spine. She was speechless; this was so much more than she'd hoped for. She knew she loved him too. He guided her to a dimly lit corner, and the dance floor slowly thinned out. Sara had long since stormed off, replaced by her father, Arnie, at the counter. But as Barry spoke, everyone else seemed to disappear. Only she and Barry continued to exist.

"Jessica," he whispered again, warm in her ear. "I've got to know—do you love me? Do you feel what I feel?"

She nodded and he tilted her chin in his hand and kissed her. They continued to dance, and her head spun, her feet barely touching the floor.

Suddenly the house lights burst on. Sara stood next to the switch-plates and glared at them with hostility. The room was nearly empty now, and right by the front door stood Todd, looking very out of place in his cowboy attire, an expression of shock and distaste on his face. He strode up to them, the heels of his boots echoing across the floor. She felt humiliated to be found with Barry like this, but then instantly grew angry to realize her brother had the power to embarrass her.

Todd stared at her hair. "It's time to go home, Jess," he spoke with rigid control.

"Whoa, cowboy," Barry said. "I'm taking the lady home tonight."

Todd stepped up to Barry, towering a good six inches over him, and quietly said, "Over my dead body—"

"Barry Bartowski!" interrupted Sara from across the room. "You're going nowhere! It's your night to clean up, remember!" Todd grabbed Jessica's arm. She looked expectantly at Barry, but he shrugged and said nothing.

As soon as they were out the door Jessica exploded. "Todd Johnson! How dare you?" she shrieked. "What right do you think you have to walk in like that and ruin my life?" She kicked the tailgate of his old blue truck.

He didn't answer, just jerked open the door and practically shoved her in. An angry silence filled the truck, and for the first time in her life she hated Todd.

4

Jessica paced back and forth in her room. She had controlled herself from stomping up the stairs, because luckily, no one else was up to cross-examine her. Besides, she wasn't particularly anxious to hear their opinions about her new hairstyle. She was incensed over Todd's intrusion into her life, but even more upsetting was the fact that he probably represented the opinion of her entire family.

She hung up the little black dress and flopped across her bed. Before long her fury was crowded out by the warm, pleasant memory of Barry's words. She replayed every phrase, every gesture, then recorded in her diary how wonderful it all made her feel.

The next morning she awoke late with an incredible headache and April tapping on her door.

"Hey, Lazy-bones, aren't you ever getting up—" April's jaw dropped. "Jessica Johnson—what in the world have you done with your hair?" April walked right in and stood before Jessica, staring in disbelief.

"Leave me alone," Jessica muttered. She crawled out of bed and looked in the mirror. Her cropped and bleached hair reminded her of the wheat field right after harvest. She ran her fingers through it and turned to April. April held her hand over her mouth, obviously suppressing laughter.

"Get out of here!" Jessica screamed. She slammed the door behind her sister-in-law and pulled on her jeans. It was too late for chores. She wondered if Todd would cover for

37

her, especially after last night's fiasco.

Another quiet knock sounded, and Jessica glanced nervously into the mirror again. She knew it was Mom. She might as well get it over with. Bracing herself, she opened the door.

Mom froze in the hallway with her eyes wide, then stiffly entered Jessica's room, closing the door behind her. She stared at Jessica with a look of complete horror.

"Jessica Victoria—your hair!" she finally gasped.

"Yes, *my* hair. It is *my* hair—so if *I* want to change it, it's *my* choice. Right?" Jessica folded her arms across her chest and stuck out her chin. Mom nodded mutely, but her eyes were misty. Jessica resented the guilt this caused her.

"I just came up to see if you wanted breakfast. Todd did your chores already. He said you needed to sleep. I thought maybe you were sick or something. . . ." She started to leave, then turned. She stood silent for a long moment, then said, "Jessica, I'll be honest. I detest what you've done to your hair. I don't understand it. Your hair was beautiful . . . before. But it's your hair, and if you like it—well, what more can I say?"

———

When Jessica came down, it was plain to see her family had been forewarned about her appearance. No one said anything as she sat down to the breakfast table. But Dad glared, hardly taking his eyes off her hair. Danny shook his head in open disgust, and Greg just snickered loudly. Jessica wondered if it was worth it. She recalled Shelly's words about exerting one's own identity, but then Shelly didn't have three brothers.

Finally, Dad threw down his napkin, mumbled something, and abruptly left the table without even finishing his breakfast.

Jessica wolfed down her food and went out to check on

Zephyr. Todd had already taken him out to pasture along with the other horses. He had cleaned and filled the water trough and even tended the hogs. Was he trying to make her feel bad? He hadn't looked at her once during breakfast.

"Jessica," Mom called from the front porch. "Better get ready for church now, dear." Jessica slowly walked over to the house. Church. She could just imagine the folks at church when they saw her hair. They'd whisper to each other in hushed tones about how sweet little Jessica must be going off the deep end. Maybe they'd want to pray for her. No thanks. She didn't need their narrow-minded criticism. No, she decided, her churchgoing days were over. Barry was right about Western religion; it was probably all just a hoax anyway. A ploy to make people feel guilty and conform to ideals that were humanly impossible.

"I'm not going, Mom," stated Jessica. She noticed Dad's bulky frame appear in the doorway. As a child he'd been her biggest supporter. When she'd wanted a horse, or to play Little League with the boys, he'd always stood by her. But would he now?

"I'm just not into this church thing anymore," she announced without looking up. She scraped the heel of her boot across the walkway, drawing a dusty line in the gravel.

"This 'church thing'?" boomed Dad, stepping out into full view. "Jessica Victoria Johnson, what in the world's come over you? I'm sorry, Betty," he told his wife. "I can't hold my tongue anymore." He turned to Jessica with a stormy face. "Jessica, as long as you live under my roof, you'll abide by my rules! And on Sunday, we go to church! Now, march upstairs and get dressed, and do something with that—that hair! Put on a hat or something!"

Jessica stomped up the porch and up to her room. She pulled on the black sleeveless dress, complete with matching hose and shoes, slicked her hair into place and marched downstairs. Her family, ready for church, was getting into various rigs, but they all paused to gape at her unusual outfit.

"Jessie, you look like a leftover beatnik," laughed Greg. "Or, I know, maybe something from an old Star Trek re-run!"

Dad glowered at Greg, then turned to Jessica. "Young lady, you go change your clothes this instant!" But Jessica didn't budge. Dad glanced at his watch—they were already late. He hit his fist on the hood of the Oldsmobile, slammed the door, and took off, spewing gravel behind him. The others followed.

The farm seemed strangely silent, but not peaceful like it used to be. Jessica swung back and forth on the porch swing. The rhythmic squeak of the chain seemed to torment her. How had things gotten so bad? Why couldn't her family accept her for who she was? Finding no convenient answers to these questions, she allowed her mind to travel a more pleasant path. She daydreamed about Barry. When would she see him again? How could she make an excuse for Todd's bad manners? The phone rang from inside and interrupted her thoughts.

"Why don't you come over, Jessie?" asked Shelly. "I've still got some of your stuff from yesterday. You could bring your suit, and we'll hang out by the pool—it's gonna be hot today."

"Sure, that sounds great!" She hung up and wished once again for her own car. Dad had promised her one next fall, after they sold the hogs. But if today were any indication, she might have a longer wait.

Todd's pickup was still parked over by the alfalfa field. He had ridden with Mom and Dad. She knew his keys would be in the ignition. The back of his pickup was stacked with hay bails he'd been about to move to the barn. It would take her hours to unload them, and besides, she'd be back before long.

Jessica and Shelly lounged by the pool, jumping in when it grew too hot. They looked at Shelly's latest fashion magazines and talked about how they were going to be the trendsetters next fall. After a while, Shelly's Mom brought them strawberry frosties in tall iced glasses.

"Shelly, your place is so cool." Really an understatement, since Jessica was totally impressed by the lavishness of the Henderson farm. Their house was modern and sprawling, with air conditioning and a built-in pool with blue tiled decks. The place was like a dream. Even their barns and horse stalls were impressive.

"Yeah, it's okay. But, Jessie, I can't stand it any longer—tell me all about Barry. I've been dying to hear. You guys were so hot together last night. You should've seen Sara Baker. I'm talking major jealousy fit!"

Jessica told Shelly about Sara's light-switch trick but was careful not to mention Todd's unexpected debut.

"Oh, and it was so weird, Jessie. I saw Todd last night just as I was leaving. Did you see him?" she giggled. "He looked so silly in all his cowboy clothes!"

To Jessica's surprise, she almost wanted to defend her brother. But she didn't. "Todd's a funny kind of guy," she said lamely.

"You said it. But he is pretty cute, and smart too. He was in my English lit. class last spring. Too bad he's such a cowboy nerd. Maybe we could turn him around. You know, like reeducate him. . . ." Jessica could see the wheels spinning in Shelly's head.

"Shelly, I better go," Jessica said when she noticed the time. "I didn't realize it's so late. Are you going to the coffeehouse tonight?"

"Uh-huh, need a ride?" Shelly leaned back into the chaise and sipped the last of her drink.

"Sure, I'd love it. Thanks for everything."

Jessica stepped on it with Todd's pickup. She wanted to make it home before her family. They always ate in town after church and usually got home just after two, but it was already two-thirty. As she sped down the road, the oil light flashed on. Just ten minutes to go. She figured it'd be okay and continued at the same speed. The light stayed on, and after just one more mile she heard a sizzling noise from the motor, followed by a loud clunk. Then the engine died. She pulled over to the side, and a foul-smelling, smokey steam poured out between the cracks of the hood. There wasn't a car in sight along the deserted strip of road. Shelly's was the only farm out this way, and likely there wouldn't be much traffic coming. She decided to walk.

It was scorching hot, and after about a mile the soles of her sandals felt like they were melting on the blazing pavement. She tried walking in the sand alongside the road, but it filled her sandals with scorching dirt that burned worse than the blacktop. After another mile, she knew she'd never make it home. If only she had stayed with the truck, at least there was shade. She turned back, angry at herself for her foolish impulsiveness, then her anger turned toward her dad. If he had gotten her a car when she turned sixteen last winter, this never would have happened.

By the time she reached Todd's pickup, her feet were blistered and her head throbbed painfully. Her mouth was paper dry and her lips cracked. She collapsed across the dusty seat.

"Jess—wake up!" Someone gently shook her. She looked up to see the wide brim of a straw cowboy hat outlined against the pale blue sky, but then it blurred.

"You okay, Jess?" It sounded like Todd. She could barely discern his face. Was that Greg behind him? Or was it just a hallucination? She tried to talk, but her throat was so parched no words could come out. They picked her up and carried her to Greg's Jeep.

"What—are you trying to kill yourself out here in this heat?" asked Greg as they headed for home. "You're flipping out on us, Jess. I think you need serious mental help." Within minutes Todd and Greg carried her up the steps into the house.

"What's wrong?" cried Mom. "Is she okay?"

"I think so," Todd answered. They laid her on the couch. It felt cool. "It's probably just the heat. Get her some water, but not too cold."

Jessica took a sip and tried to speak, but the words came out in a hoarse whisper. "Thanks Todd . . . Greg." Mom took over and wiped her down with a cool washcloth and gave her lemonade with a straw. It reminded Jessica of when she had chickenpox. She soon fell asleep.

———————

When Jessica awoke, it was in her own bed with the drapes drawn and the soft whirring sound of the fan in her doorway. She stretched and looked at her little alarm clock—6:38. Shelly was coming at seven! Jessica quickly dressed and went downstairs.

"How are you feeling, honey?" Mom asked with concern in her eyes.

"Pretty good now. I think that rest was just what I needed. I told Shelly I'd go to town with her tonight," Jessica announced, trying to sound light and cheerful, as if nothing out of the ordinary had happened today.

"I don't think so, missy," Dad called from the living room. He folded his paper and walked into the kitchen. "I've got a few things to discuss with you first. For starters, you're grounded." Jessica moaned and slumped into a vinyl kitchen chair. "And it looks like we need to review some house rules around here, young lady. Curfew, for instance, has not changed. It's still midnight on weekends and ten the rest of the week in the summer. And I guess I need to remind you about our dating rule. Do you recall you're not to go out with anyone we haven't met? Or did you forget? And now for a new rule. From now on, that Blue Skye joint is *off* limits."

Jessica glared at him. Her father had suddenly turned into a tyrannical dictator. He was treating her like an infant.

"Now regarding Todd's pickup—you've got some explaining to do, Jessica. Todd, will you come down here?" Dad called up the stairway. Todd came into the kitchen, hands in his pockets and head down. Dad continued. "Tell your sister the verdict on your truck."

"Well, the engine's pretty much shot. Fried, that is. Other than that, it's fine." He laughed sarcastically without looking at Jessica.

She stared at the floor. She had never meant to hurt Todd. But was it really her fault the pickup broke down?

"So, what do you intend to do about it?" asked Dad.

Jessica shrugged her shoulders. "Maybe I could pay to fix it. How much will it cost?"

Todd laughed again, but he wasn't a very convincing cynic. "Well, a rebuilt engine would run about seven hundred—that's if I did some of the work myself."

"You got that much, Jessie?" Dad asked.

She shook her head. Including her savings, she'd be lucky to scrape up one hundred, especially after her recent shopping spree.

"Well, I had put aside about that much for the down-payment for your car, Jessie. Now I guess we'll have to use it for Todd's new engine."

"That's not fair!" she exclaimed. "The guys all got their cars at sixteen! Dad, you promised!"

"Was it fair for you to take your brother's truck while it was overloaded with hay, and then go hot-rodding over to your friend's in the heat of the day? You didn't even ask Todd."

"Well, it's not fair for you to ground me and not even let me go to the one place in Poloma that interests me." She decided to change the subject. "Why are you treating me like a child?"

"That's exactly how you're acting, Jessica. For starters—look what you did to your hair. And breaking curfew, and the people you're with—"

"There's nothing wrong with my friends!"

"Ha, that's what you think," Greg called from the back porch as he wiped grease off his hands. "I've been asking around town, and rumor has it drugs are coming out of that joint. I think it's just a matter of time until the sheriff shuts it down altogether."

"That's a big fat lie!"

"I doubt it. And I'll bet that looney-toon guitar-player friend of yours is at the bottom of it. There's something shifty about that guy. I don't trust him a bit."

Jessica threw a look of accusation at Todd. He must have told them about her and Barry. He evenly returned her gaze, but his eyes looked hurt. Maybe he hadn't told, but it was just a matter of time. The worst part of this whole confrontation was that she couldn't see Barry tonight! Somehow she had to get around it.

"You can't treat me this way, Dad! I'm almost grown up. What are you going to do, lock me in my room?"

"I probably should, at least until you come back to your senses. Come on, Jessica, you've got to know this is for your own good."

"Yeah, Jess, we don't want to see you get messed up with the wrong people," said Todd.

"Sure, and you guys are such experts! You're all so narrow and bigoted, I can't believe you're my own family! Well, you can try, but you can't run my life!" Angry tears stung her eyelids, and she stormed upstairs. She wouldn't give them the pleasure of seeing her cry. She threw herself across her bed and sobbed.

The sound of a vehicle pulling in the driveway drew her to the window. It was Shelly. Jessica watched Todd walk over to her. She hoped he would make some good excuse about why she couldn't go. He leaned against Shelly's Blazer for what seemed like a long time. Jessica wondered what on earth they could be talking about. Then to her amazement, Todd hopped into the Blazer and rode off with Shelly. Well, maybe Todd would discover the Blue Skye wasn't such a bad place after all.

Her thoughts turned to Barry. Had he tried to call today? Would he look for her tonight? If she knew his phone number, she could call, but she didn't want to call him at the Blue Skye. She didn't want to hear Sara's acidic voice telling her he was busy. She decided to write him a letter. Barry was the kind of guy who'd appreciate a well-written note. She poured out her heart to him, page after page.

———

The next day she was dying to know what Todd thought about the Blue Skye, but couldn't ask. She'd decided the best punishment for her family would be the silent treatment. She did her daily chores, then retreated to her room, even skipping meals just to make them worry. She thought about Zephyr wanting a ride to the pond, but she couldn't leave the house. Barry might call.

By Wednesday, Shelly phoned to invite her to the coffeehouse, and Jessica made a feeble excuse, unwilling to mention her juvenile grounding.

"Well, Jessie," Shelly said on the phone. "Barry asked about you again last night. Sara's really trying to get him back. So far he hasn't acted very interested, but you better not waste too much time. He's pretty hot stuff, you know."

The week passed slowly. Still nothing. No word, no calls from Barry. By Friday, she felt desperate to see him. Why hadn't he even called? Surely he had received her letter by now. She wished she'd never sent it. It probably scared him off.

Finally, she'd had it with her waiting vigil. She decided to take Zephyr for a ride. On her way out to the barn, she noticed a strange pink van pull into the driveway. She walked over to investigate. A young man hopped out with a long white florist box tied with a big red bow.

"Flowers for Jessica Johnson," he announced.

Jessica thanked him and eagerly opened the package. Roses! Six long-stemmed red roses. She ripped open the card and read, "For my Jessica. A rose for each day I haven't seen your lovely face. Where have you been? I miss you. Come tonight. Love, Barry."

Jessica hugged the roses. He still cared! She dashed into the kitchen to put them in water. April was sitting at the table peeling potatoes.

"My, my—red roses. This sounds serious, Jessie," teased April. "Who's the admirer? Anyone I know?"

Though happy, Jessica wasn't ready to abandon her silent treatment yet. She mutely filled a glass vase and carefully arranged her roses, then took them upstairs. Her room had become much too familiar lately, and much too confining, but it was the only place she felt safe from peering eyes and insensitive remarks.

She had to see him tonight. She decided to call Shelly, and they arranged to meet on the main road at eight. She knew it would be tricky to get away unseen, but it was her only chance and a risk she must take.

Jessica silently cleaned up the supper dishes and straightened the kitchen. This helped alleviate some guilt for what she was about to do.

"Thanks, Jessica," Mom said. "I know you're not speaking to anyone these days, but I hope you can still listen. I'm sorry you're taking this so hard, but you must realize we love you and we're doing this for your own good."

Jessica said nothing. She hung up the dish towel and went upstairs. For her own good! What made them such experts? If they had their way, they'd probably lock her up until she turned twenty-one!

Jessica watched Greg and Todd leave for the movies. Danny and April were resting in their room, and Mom and Dad were watching an old John Wayne movie downstairs.

She dressed carefully, then sneaked down the back stairway and out the back door. It was almost eight as she jogged through the alfalfa field in front of the house. She emerged on the main road just as Shelly's Blazer came into sight. She envied Shelly's freedom. Her parents would never treat their daughter this way.

"What's the deal meeting me on the road like this?" Shelly asked suspiciously as Jessica hopped in. "Why didn't you want me to pull in?"

"Oh, my parents were getting a little uptight about me going to the Blue Skye so much, you know."

"Yeah, I know what you mean. My dad keeps warning me it's a big cover-up for drug trafficking. Ha! What a bunch of paranoids—just because they don't understand, they think the worst. They watch too much TV—if you ask me. I've never seen any drugs, or even booze for that matter. If our parents only knew how other kids are out drinking and partying. All we're doing is just having coffee and listening to some new philosophies, and they throw fits. I don't get it!"

Jessica nodded. Parents were impossible to understand.

5

*B*arry's voice was low and meaningful as he read a poem on homelessness. Jessica considered her comfortable home with a strange feeling of guilt. Suddenly the idea of indigence had a peculiar appeal. Barry finished, and the crowd grew hushed. He took up his guitar and began to softly pick, and Jessica grew mesmerized by his music. She watched his fingers skim over the strings. She felt proud of him. More than that, she felt love for him rushing through her, warm and strong.

After his song, he disappeared into the back room. Jessica waited, glancing over her shoulder occasionally, but he didn't return. Shelly was deep in conversation with an older guy Jessica vaguely recalled from school. Jessica slipped away from the table unnoticed.

"Bartowski, I've had it with you!" exclaimed Sara's dad, Arnie Baker, his back to the barely cracked door. He continued in an outraged tone. "And I've had it with your lies and games! I asked you out here to help me, not to drag me down to your despicable level! I won't put up with it—"

Jessica backed away from the door, but not soon enough. Barry had seen her. Her cheeks burned in embarrassment, and what a horrid conversation to overhear. She hadn't meant to.

She sat next to Shelly, confused and worried. Why was Arnie being so awful? Did Barry's philosophy disturb Arnie? Well, what about freedom of speech? Or was it because

Barry no longer returned the affections of his daughter? Had Sara complained to her daddy? Jessica grew even more indignant toward Arnie's treatment of Barry.

Just then someone touched her arm, and she turned to face him. Barry's dark eyes met hers and she detected pain behind them. "Come with me," he whispered.

She followed him impulsively, out the back door and down the alley. He led her through a dark rear entrance and up some dingy stairs behind the Silver Bull Saloon. The tiny apartment was hot and stuffy; noise from the tavern below seeped through the floor. Her heart pounded madly and something inside warned her to flee. This was all wrong! But her feet wouldn't move, and all she could think of was the fiery sensation that burned inside her chest.

Trying to compose herself, she took a breath and glanced around the apartment. It was no bigger than her bedroom and fairly neat, but a sickening-sweet musty odor clung to the air. It must be incense. She'd smelled it burning at the boutique she and Shelly had shopped at.

"Sit down," he pulled her over to a decrepit-looking chair, then sank down onto the edge of the bed. His head slumped and his sleek brown hair fell across his face. She stared at him in uncomfortable silence, studying his shoulders hunched over in dejection. He looked up slowly, and she thought she saw tears.

"I had to see you one last time, Jessica. . . ."

"What do you mean 'one last time'?"

"I'm leaving, Jessica—you saw Arnie tonight. He's sacking me."

"But why?" she asked. "Because of your views? Your philosophy? Is it because he doesn't agree with you?" Barry stared at her with a puzzled expression, then reached over and pulled her from the chair and into his arms.

"Oh, Jessica," he breathed. "You see so much. You've been so special to me. I've never known anyone like you."

He held her close, and when he kissed her she thought she'd dissolve in his arms. How could this be? How could he be leaving now? Just when they'd really found each other.

"You can't go," she pleaded. "I'll be lost without you."

He kissed her again and held her face in his hands. "I know. I'll be lost without you, too. We only have right now—" He pulled her closer and she felt dizzy. Her world was spinning out of orbit. Everything she'd believed since childhood slipped away in his warm embrace.

A loud knocking jerked her back to reality. Barry froze, clamping his hand over her mouth.

"Open the door, Bartowski! We know you're in there!" With horror, Jessica recognized Greg's voice.

"Open up or we'll break it down!" yelled her other brother Danny.

Jessica wanted to die. It was like a horrible nightmare. Barry's hand slipped from her mouth and he walked to the door and flipped off the lock in defeat. She wanted to stop him. But already her three brothers had filled the tiny room. Greg looked at Barry, and without a single word punched him full-force in the stomach. Barry curled over and staggered to the bed. He clutched his middle and moaned.

Jessica rushed to him, but Danny and Greg blocked her way, then physically hauled her from the room. Todd glanced at her with what might have been sympathy, but she clenched her teeth and turned her face away. Todd was a traitor. She didn't want his pity. She fought all three of them, kicking and screaming down the stairs. An overly made-up woman staggered to the hallway and gaped at the four of them. Jessica glared back, then kicked harder. How dare her brothers treat her like this!

Danny and Greg took turns lecturing all the way home, but she tuned them out and fumed in silence. Her hatred toward them overwhelmed her. She grew angrier with each mile. She'd never forgive them—not in a hundred years!

Back at home she refused to budge from the back of Greg's Jeep, and Danny reached in to pull her out.

"Get your dirty hands off me!" she seethed. She leaped down and stomped into the house.

"Well, at least she can still talk," Greg said with a mocking laugh.

Jessica burst through the front door and started for her room, but Dad cut her off. He loomed before her, feet straddled, hands folded across his chest.

"Just a minute, young lady. First, you march into the living room and cool off. Then we'll talk."

Jessica sized him up. His face was dark and intense. She'd never seen him look quite like that. She decided resistance was futile, especially with her brothers huddled by the door. She flopped on the couch and listened while Greg told Dad where they had found her, painting the picture even worse than it was.

"Jessica Victoria!" Dad growled with clenched fists. "I don't know what to do with you! You've defied me. And with that—that no-good druggy Bartowski!" He turned on his heel and stormed into the kitchen, slamming the door behind him.

Todd stepped into the living room. "Jess," he whispered. "Don't you know what you're doing to yourself? Can't you see that Bartowski's bad news? Greg just heard he's suspected of drug peddling. The police will probably pick him up soon."

Jessica glared at Todd without answering. She didn't care if Barry was suspected of murder. He was better than this family. She pushed past Todd toward the stairs, but the words coming from the kitchen stopped her. She paused by the closed kitchen door and listened as Dad continued speaking to Mom in a low but angry voice, obviously unaware of an eavesdropper.

"Jessie's just like her mother. I don't know what to with

her. Susan was the same way—stubborn, headstrong, bent for ruin! I can't stand to see it happening all over again!"

Jessica stared at her brothers in confusion. They appeared equally perplexed. Except maybe Danny—he scratched his head, almost as if he vaguely remembered something.

"Oh, honey," her mother said in an artificial voice. "This has nothing to do with Susan. Jessie's just going through a stage, a phase—"

Jessica could stand it no longer. What in the world did they mean? She flung open the kitchen door and stood before them.

"What are you talking about? What do you mean, 'just like her mother'? Who is Susan?" Mom and Dad both looked horrified. Dad sunk into a kitchen chair and covered his face with his hands. She'd never in all her life seen him like this.

"Nothing, dear," Mom said in a high-pitched voice, then turned to the sink. "You must've heard wrong. Besides, you shouldn't eavesdrop." She ran the tap into the empty sink. It just kept running and running—for no apparent reason.

Jessica looked from one parent to the other, and then over to her brothers hanging anxiously in the door. A thick, heavy silence hung in the air. Jessica felt like she couldn't breathe.

"What's going on? Tell me!" she demanded in a shrill voice that sounded like someone else. She looked at Danny, and his gaze dropped. She turned and glared at Dad, then practically screamed, "What did you mean, Dad? Tell me!"

"Hush, Jessica," said Mom. She shut off the faucet and slowly wiped her hands on a dish towel. "Don't get all worked up." Mom's face was pale and drawn, and Jessica could see her hands shaking. Mom sent a look of inquiry to Dad. First he stared blankly, then solemnly nodded.

"Sit down, Jessica," Mom said. "You boys might as well listen too. This is something you all should hear." She clasped her hands and took a deep breath. "Something we probably should have talked about long before this." She sat down and sighed. "Danny, you may even remember some of this, you were almost six. . . ." They sat around the table with a mixture of somber and puzzled expressions.

"Is this about Aunt Susan?" asked Danny.

Mom nodded, cleared her throat, and began. She spoke mechanically, in short, stilted sentences as if she were reading a script. "Jessica, do you remember Grandma Jeannette? You knew she wasn't Dad's real mother. She married Grandpa after Dad's mother passed on. Jeannette had a daughter. Dad's stepsister. Her name is Susan. Susan's about ten years younger than Dad. She was miserable after moving from Kansas City to Poloma. She became very rebellious, ran around with all the wild kids. Finally, she wound up pregnant right before her senior year. She had a baby in January."

Mom looked at Jessica with sad eyes. "Susan wanted to leave Kansas. She wanted a new life. Ironically, I was pregnant at the same time. But I lost my baby. It seemed funny then—Susan having a perfectly healthy baby girl when she didn't even want it, and me losing mine. . . . When she offered us her baby, it was like a gift from God. And I'd wanted a girl so badly. She made us promise never to contact her or tell anyone of the adoption. Susan wanted her child to grow up as a Johnson—with no stigma as an outsider."

Jessica couldn't believe it. This baby they were talking about was her! She shook her head, trying to stop the ringing in her ears. Confusing thoughts tumbled in her mind like a hopelessly tangled snarl of string. Would she ever be able to sort it out again?

"The timing was so incredible, Jessica," Mom continued. "We knew it was God's design. I'd miscarried within a week of your birth . . . and then to have a girl—after three boys. We adopted you gladly, Jessica. And we've always thought of you as our own." Mom had tears in her eyes.

Jessica heard the words and tried to take it all in, but all she could think of was how they had deceived her. Everyone stared at her expectantly. What did they want her to say? Thank you very much? She stared at the old box fan by the back door. Its blades were whirling round and round. She could almost follow them with her eyes. The sound blended with the buzzing in her head. It was all too strange.

"I'm not your daughter," she said flatly.

Mom shook her head. "Maybe not by blood, but we've always considered you—"

"Then all these years, my life's been nothing but a lie!" Jessica stood and placed her hands on the table, trying to steady herself. The buzzing in her head had become a loud roar, and she had to yell to hear herself above the noise. "And you're not even related to me? None of you? What a joke! What a cruel and horrible joke! Were you *ever* going to tell me? You'd let me just go on—believing this lie?" She stared in wonder, as if seeing them all for the first time. This wasn't even her family! She didn't belong to them! She dashed from the kitchen to her room, ignoring their pleas to return.

Her head throbbed as she cried into her pillow. Her life as Jessica Johnson was over! As though someone had sneaked in and stolen it while her back was turned. Even Barry was leaving. She broke into fresh sobs at the memory of Barry's face when Greg slugged him. The way his eyes had locked into hers while he was in pain. Life was completely unjust! She cried until the tears wouldn't come. At last she was rescued by a fitful sleep.

———

Jessica opened her eyes to darkness and knew someone had been in her room. Her bedspread had been laid over her. She rose from her bed not fully awake and walked to her open window. She tried to breathe in the scent of the earth. She wanted the evening breeze to cleanse her, to wipe away the events of the day. Pale moonlight washed over the fields in a soft colorless light. It used to be one of her favorite sights. It used to be a time when she spoke to God, whispering thanks for all His good gifts. She used to feel hope for what the future might hold as she would look out over their land. But now she felt empty—flat. This was no longer *her* farm. No longer *her* family. She had no one!

Suddenly she longed for Barry with an urgency. Had he already left town? She remembered Todd saying the police would question Barry. She had to warn him! He had to get away! The answer was clear—she would leave with him. There was nothing left here for her anyway.

She packed a small bag. She had about thirty dollars in her purse, but that wouldn't get her far. She remembered the antique cookie jar on top of the china cabinet. Everyone knew Dad stashed spare cash there, but no one ever touched it. Maybe it wasn't stealing. After all, with her gone they'd save money. Silently she emptied the pear-shaped jar, stuffing the bills into her bag without pausing to count.

Once outside, she wondered how to get to town. The noise of taking a rig from the driveway would surely wake someone. Far off, on the edge of the east field, sat the old flatbed. It could take her to town. The wind blew from the west, and hopefully no one would hear the engine way out there. She ran through the field and waded across the creek. Her heart pounded, more from fear than exertion. She must escape! She heard something and crouched down in the uncut grain, listening for footsteps. But it was only a horse. She recognized Zephyr's familiar whinny from the nearby pasture. Her heart twisted in pain, but she continued to run.

He was no longer her horse. Because she was no longer the farmer's daughter.

At last she reached the truck. Her side ached painfully, but it was a good pain. It distracted her from the ache in her heart as she chose to abandon the only home, the only life she'd ever known. . . .

What if he's already gone? she worried as she drove toward town. She would've gone faster, but the old flatbed might disintegrate at a higher speed. At last she pulled into the back lot of the Silver Bull. It was dark with no one about as she slipped up the narrow stairway and knocked lightly on Barry's door. No answer. Had he left already? She knocked again, louder this time, calling his name. The door cracked open. Then it opened wider, and Barry yanked her in.

"Are you crazy?" he demanded. "Why did you come back, Jessica? Your brothers will kill me this time. Go on— go home to them. Stay away from me—you hear!" Jessica couldn't believe her ears. This didn't sound like the Barry she knew.

"I-I just came to warn you, the police will be coming for you. I heard they're going to take you in for questioning. That's all I had to say. If you want me to leave, I will." She looked down at the matted green rug beneath her feet, uncertain of whether to stay or go. The silence in the stuffy room was more suffocating than the air. She wondered if she could handle his rejection. She knew she couldn't go back home.

"I thought you loved me, Barry," she whispered. "I left home to run away with you." Her words were bolder than she felt, but they were out now. She glanced uncomfortably around the room, not wanting to see his face. Her eyes stopped on the shabby dresser. Spread across the top were plastic baggies and containers. She wondered what they were for, but Barry interrupted her thoughts.

"How far do you think we'd get before they came looking, Jessica? Don't you think those cowboy brothers of yours would hunt us down like dogs?"

"They're *not* my brothers," she announced with no sign of emotion. "I found out tonight—none of them are even my family. I was adopted. I have no one." She turned to leave. Maybe she'd been wrong about Barry.

Barry put his hand on the door and pulled her toward him. "Wait, Jessica. I'm sorry." He looked hard into her eyes. "Would you really run away with me?"

She nodded but felt a trace of uncertainty.

"We better leave right now. It's almost three A.M. That doesn't give us much time to hide our trail before morning." He stuffed his things into pillowcases and bags.

"Here, you take these bags to that little blue Volvo in the parking lot. I'll be right down." He shoved the keys into her hand.

She found his car and tossed in their stuff. She considered moving the flatbed to conceal her whereabouts, but she knew they'd figure it out sooner or later. Barry dashed down with a small suitcase, which he carefully placed in the trunk, laying the rest of their things on top. He hopped in with a bright smile.

"This is exciting, Jessica. You and me on the run. Hope you like to drive fast, 'cause we need to make good time."

They sped down the wide-open highway. Jessica couldn't read the speedometer but knew she'd never traveled so fast. She'd never flown in a plane, but this had to be close. The straight road stretched before them like a ribbon of silver, lit by the full moon. Suddenly Poloma seemed like a lifetime away.

"Better get some sleep, Jessica. I'll need you to give me a break in a few hours." He inserted a tape and Jessica drifted off to the sound of classical guitar.

———————

When Jessica awoke, it was already light, and she sensed by the traffic noises that they were driving through a city. She didn't move or show she was awake. Suddenly the situation felt very frightening. Her chest constricted in panic. What had she done? Her stomach rumbled, but she continued to slump against the door, pretending to sleep. Her neck ached and she longed to stretch, but she couldn't bring herself to talk to him. The reality stunned her. She peeked out with one eye to see the bright morning sun exposing the dusty, dingy interior of Barry's old car.

Well, it was too late for regret. She couldn't look back now. She glanced over at Barry, still without moving. Dark circles hung under his eyes, and his face looked gaunt and sallow. He was probably exhausted. Finally, her neck could stand it no longer. She sat up and stretched.

"Where are we, Barry?"

"Well, Dorothy, we're not in Kansas anymore," he announced lightly. "Welcome to Tulsa, Oklahoma, Jessica."

"Cool. I've never been here." She looked at the tall buildings in amazement. "Can we stop for a bite? I brought money, Barry. And I don't expect for you to pay my way." She wanted to make it perfectly clear from the start. She wouldn't tie him down. Hopefully he had brought her because he loved her.

"I don't want to take any chance of being seen just yet. So as much as I hate it, we'll have to go through a McDonald's drive-through. Just don't ever tell anyone that Barry Bartowski actually consumed an Egg McMuffin!" He laughed cynically. But Jessica was glad. McDonald's sounded good to her. Outside of town, they pulled into the Golden Arches, and she ordered several breakfast items.

"You always eat that much?" Barry asked as he entered the busy freeway. She nodded with her mouth full.

Later that morning, she relieved him from driving, and he slept in the backseat. He had instructed her to continue south-west, to stick to the highway and avoid the Interstate. She didn't know their exact destination but didn't question him. He seemed to have it all worked out, and she decided she had to trust his judgment.

The little Volvo was quite a change from their big farm rigs. It was fun feeling close to the ground and hugging the occasional curves on the country road. She enjoyed the scenery while Barry slept. Oklahoma looked similar to Kansas, only the farms appeared to grow a larger variety of crops. The weather was perfect for traveling. Last week's heat wave seemed to have evaporated, and the smell of freshly cut hay breezed into the open windows. Jessica's doubts and worries began to vanish. Maybe she was doing the right thing after all. She decided not to think about home. She had no home. Instead she should enjoy the exhilaration of her new-found freedom.

By afternoon they encountered cattle country, and before long a road sign announced they were entering Texas. It reminded her of Greg. He'd been here last summer for a rodeo. She thought of her family, then remembered they weren't her family anymore. She didn't want to think of them. But she couldn't help but wonder. Were they upset and worried? Could they possibly be relieved to have her gone?

Barry stirred in the backseat.

"Where are we, Jessica?" he asked groggily.

"Just entering Texas," she answered proudly.

"You're kidding?" He bolted up, leaning over the seat. "Have you checked the gas gauge?"

She gulped and looked down to discover the needle solidly on 'E.' "Oh Barry, I'm so sorry. I didn't think—"

"Well, if you want to live in the grown-up world, you'd better start thinking!" His words stung.

"That sign says Grover, five miles," she offered hopefully. "Do you think we'll make it?"

"Maybe. . . . But Jessica, you've got to pay attention to things like gas gauges. You're not a little girl anymore." She nodded and wished he'd lighten up. They made it to Grover, and she paid for the gas in order to ease her conscience. They took a quick stroll through the little town and stopped at an old-fashioned grocery store to get some items for lunch.

"I'll drive now," Barry announced as he climbed behind the wheel. "By the way, we're heading for Dallas. I've got family there. Not actually in Dallas, but close by. We should be there in just over an hour."

"I thought you were from New York."

"Well I am—sort of. I lived there awhile, but my family's mostly here."

Jessica never dreamed Barry came from another form of "Cowboy Country." Especially after he'd been so arrogant about Kansas, she never would've thought. . . .

"How come you don't talk like a Texan, then?"

He laughed. "I worked hard to lose that accent, but I can still do it—I just don't care to."

"Tell me about your family."

His face grew grim, and Jessica wished she hadn't asked. "You'll find out soon enough," was all he said.

They drove in silence. What kind of mysterious family did he have? Before, when she had tried to imagine him with a family, it had always been with a professor-type dad in a tweed jacket probably smoking a pipe, and a sensitive artistic mom who enjoyed classical music, with perhaps a couple of congenial, intelligent siblings tossed in for good measure. She leaned back, closed her eyes, and wondered. . . .

"Wake up, Jessica," said Barry. "We're almost home— well, I guess you could call it that."

6

$\mathcal{B}$arry left the freeway just outside of Dallas and continued in silence.

Jessica noticed his fingers tighten on the steering wheel and his jaw grow firm. Her insides churned, partly in anticipation, but also with fear. The awful realization of running away was hitting her again—this time it gripped her heart like an iron vise.

"Barry, I'm scared." A renegade tear slid down her cheek and she swiped it away with the back of her hand.

"Don't worry, Jessica," he assured. "Everything'll be okay." She looked over at him and he smiled. She felt better. Barry would take care of her.

He turned the car into what looked to be an old housing development, then drove down a couple streets with run-down tract homes and finally parked in front of a particularly shabby-looking house. Two huge motorcycles were parked importantly on the dry, brown front lawn, and a snarling pitbull jerked from his chain that was tied to the porch. Jessica looked at Barry in bewilderment.

"This is it," he said with apparent indifference. "Now do you understand why I ran away at sixteen?" She couldn't believe it. This place was nothing like Barry. Were they going to actually stay here?

"Don't worry, Jessica, this is just a quick stopover." He gave the feisty dog a wide berth and led Jessica through the garage. It reeked like a filthy cat-litter box, but she saw no cats. Although they could have been hiding anywhere amidst the clutter of decaying boxes, old newspapers, and bags of garbage. She held her breath while Barry opened the door, then followed him inside, gasping for air. But the dingy interior of the house smelled no better, perhaps worse. A moldy, putrid odor mixed with stale cigarette smoke permeated the house. The kitchen floor felt sticky and gritty beneath her feet, and dirty dishes that obviously had been sitting there for a long time lined the counters. The house had an abandoned look and the curtains and drapes were drawn. Jessica wondered if anyone actually lived there.

"Mom?" Barry called. He flipped a light switch to illuminate even more filth and neglect. Jessica cringed. She did not want stay in this dump! They heard a moan from down the hall and followed it to discover a sickly woman in the back bedroom.

"Hi, Mom," Barry said in a flat, monotone voice. He didn't enter the room, but hung back in the doorway. The woman propped herself on a skinny elbow and peered at them.

"It's me. Don't you even recognize your own son?" She coughed and pulled the red crushed-velvet bedspread to her chin. Next to her bed, ashtrays overflowed, trash littered the floor, and a variety of pills and bottles lined her dresser.

"I'm not well, Barry," she said in a raspy voice.

"So what else is new, Mom?" he remarked without sympathy. Jessica looked at him in surprise. "She's always like this, Jessica," he said to her, as if his mother were deaf. "She's lived with little red pills to get her going and little yellow pills to mellow her out, a bottle of cheap whiskey to make her feel good and three packs of cigarettes a day. Right Mom? Or have you cut back? It's amazing she's still alive."

Jessica stared speechlessly at the scrawny woman. Dark eyes protruded from her skeleton-like face in a sad, subhuman way, and yet they still held a flicker of lucidity.

"I'm Jessica Johnson," she said bravely, waiting for a further introduction. She glanced at Barry. He stared blankly across the room as if his mother were invisible.

The woman coughed and cleared her throat. "I'm Celeste Bartowski, and my son lacks manners. Come closer so I can get a better look at you." Barry tugged on Jessica's arm, as if to hold her back. But she resisted him and approached Celeste. Barry grumbled and walked away.

"Pretty girl," commented Celeste. "What Barry said is mostly true. I am a mess—" She coughed again. Deep, racking coughs hunched her body over in pain, and she sat up wheezing, tears in her eyes.

"Do you need a drink of water?" Jessica offered with growing concern. Celeste nodded breathlessly, and Jessica hurried back to the kitchen to scavenge for an uncontaminated glass. Finding none, she spotted the cleanest one and washed it with hot, soapy water.

Barry was back in the hallway again, leaning on the doorframe, his arms folded across his chest. He surveyed his mother with an air of indifference.

"Where's Wade?" he asked. "Isn't that his chopper out front?" Jessica stepped past him and handed his mother the water.

Celeste took a long, slow drink. "He and Snake came by to pick up my car—to fix the radiator—so he can sell it for me." She took a breath. It was plain to see she was weak.

"Knowing Wade, he'll probably strip it and bring it back next year," laughed Barry.

Celeste frowned. "At least Wade is around to help me out while I'm dying," she said with another deep cough.

"Mom, you've been dying ever since I've known you." Barry turned on his heel and left again.

Jessica sighed in exasperation. How could he treat his mother like this? But then she remembered she had just run away from her mother. Of course, she wasn't really her mother. Would it ever sink in?

"Celeste, what's wrong?" asked Jessica. "Why are you so ill?" It was none of her business, but somehow she'd already begun to care for this pitiful scrap of a woman.

Celeste leaned her head back on the dingy, grayed pillowcase and stared up at the ceiling, as if she were looking far away. "Emphysema," she answered. "The doctor told me last Christmas I wouldn't see Spring." She coughed again, and suddenly Jessica longed to run from this repulsive place. But Celeste's pain-stricken eyes held Jessica's gaze, and her feet remained planted on the stained shag carpet.

"Who cares for you?" Jessica asked, suddenly filled with unexpected indignation. How could this poor woman possibly care for herself in her deteriorated condition?

Celeste made a cackling sound, almost a laugh. "Care for me? Mostly no one. My insurance ran out long ago, so I can't go to the hospital—not that I want to. I'd rather just die . . . here. The sooner the better." Celeste turned to the wall, and Jessica stood and stared hopelessly at the hunched-over back of the faded pink nightgown. Then she noticed the more even but shallow breathing and realized Celeste was probably asleep.

She tiptoed out to find Barry, but he wasn't in the house. She looked outside to see that the Volvo was gone. Where was he? And how dare he leave her stranded here? Suddenly she felt suffocated and realized her lungs were filled with that foul, stagnant air. She'd always considered herself to be pretty strong when it came to bad smells. She could clean up after horses and cows, and even pigs, but this was something entirely different. Jerking back the greasy drapes, she threw open the windows and the sultry afternoon heat poured in, but with it came fresh air. She breathed deeply, then turned in frustration at the squalor surrounding her.

Jessica rolled up her sleeves and attacked the kitchen with a vengeance. Well, she knew how to work, and her fury at Barry fueled her into high speed. She washed, scrubbed, scoured, and straightened, until at last it looked like a kitchen. More than three hours had lapsed during her cleaning rampage, yet Barry did not return.

Celeste awoke, and Jessica coaxed some chicken bouillon down her, the only edible thing she'd found in the entire kitchen. Then she tidied Celeste's bedroom. She longed to rip the filthy sheets from her bed, and perhaps even burn them.

"Jessica, can you help me to the bathroom?" asked Celeste. Jessica nodded and eased Celeste up. She was so light and fragile, Jessica thought she could carry her if necessary.

"Thank you, dear," Celeste wheezed as she shut the bathroom door.

Jessica searched the tiny linen closet and found crisp clean sheets, almost like new, tucked way in the back. She wondered what Celeste could possibly be saving them for. With marathon speed, she stripped the bed and even flipped the mattress, replacing the sheets and plumping the pillows.

"Jessica?" Celeste called from the bathroom.

"Coming," Jessica replied, almost out of breath.

"Jessica, I'd love to take a bath," Celeste said wistfully. "Would you mind—could you help me?"

Jessica didn't know what to say. She'd never helped anyone with a bath before, other than livestock or their dog, Betsy, after a wallow in the mud. She stared down at her feet, then at the dirty tub.

"Okay, Celeste. You sit and rest, and I'll get it ready." Jessica lowered the lid on the rickety toilet seat and helped Celeste sit down. She located some cleanser and an old hard sponge beneath the sink, then quickly scrubbed and filled the tub with warm water. An old container of foaming bath oil sat high on a shelf. "Is this any good, Celeste?" she asked, opening the dusty bottle and sniffing it. "Umm, violets. Should I pour some in?" Celeste nodded.

The tub now full, Jessica looked at Celeste questionably. Celeste stood shakily and unbuttoned her gown. It fell to the floor in a limp heap. Jessica suppressed a groan and turned away. Celeste looked like a human skeleton. It reminded her of those awful black-and-white photos of holocaust victims. She clenched her teeth and gently supported a bony arm to ease Celeste into the tub of sweet-smelling bubbles.

"Ahh," Celeste sighed as she sank into the water. "Blissful . . . I haven't had a tub bath in ages." She leaned her head back. "I've always loved the scent of violets. It reminds me of something my mother used to say. Let's see, it goes something like, 'Forgiveness is like the fragrance of violets on the heel of the one who tread them.' "

Jessica considered those words as she gently shampooed Celeste's thin, dark hair. There wasn't a strand of gray in it.

"How old are you, Celeste?" She blotted Celeste's hair with a hand towel.

"Forty-six," sighed Celeste.

Jessica was astonished. That was younger than her mom—her adopted mom, anyway. But Celeste seemed so old.

After a while the water started to cool, and Jessica helped Celeste from the tub, draping a towel around her and setting her on the seat of the toilet.

"I'll get you something to put on," Jessica called as she dashed back to the bedroom. She dug through the bulky Mediterranean-style dresser until she found a silky nightgown of pale lavender. "How's this?" she asked, holding up the pretty gown.

"I forgot all about that. I was saving it—" murmured Celeste, followed by that odd hollow laugh. Jessica slipped the gown over her head anyway.

"This feels nice," Celeste whispered. She stroked the satiny fabric. Jessica guided her back and tucked her into the clean bed, then stepped back in satisfaction, not knowing what more to do.

"Clean sheets. . . . Thanks, Jessica. Are you an angel in disguise?"

Jessica laughed. "Hardly. Now get some rest, Celeste. You need anything?"

Celeste shook her head and smiled. When she smiled she looked much younger, almost like a girl.

Jessica gazed outside at the remnants of a rosy sunset slowly being devoured by an ebony sky. It was getting late, and Barry was still gone. She felt hungry and tired and wondered where she should sleep. There were two other small bedrooms. One was stripped bare of everything except a twin bed with a stained naked mattress. The other looked like someone's room—maybe this Wade that Barry had mentioned. She dug around until she found more sheets, then made up the bed in the empty room. The only thing that seemed to keep her mind off of her trouble was to keep working. She remembered how her mother—Betty—used to do the same thing. Jessica scrubbed the bathroom and loaded the dirty laundry in the washer. To her amazement there was actually some detergent in the bottom of an old box. Still no Barry. Had he abandoned her for good?

She searched the barren kitchen cupboards again. How had Celeste survived? A car pulled up, and Jessica peeked out to see an old black Thunderbird parked in the driveway. Out climbed a large, burly man with a scruffy beard. His black leather vest trimmed in metal gaped across a bulging belly, and his jeans were smeared with dark, greasy dirt. He strolled up the walk followed by a skinny man with long, stringy hair. The ugly pitbull on the porch didn't even bark. Then to her horror, without knocking, both of the strange men walked right into Celeste's house.

"Who are you?" asked the big guy in a gruff voice. She backed into the kitchen, grasping behind her for the drawer she knew contained at least one knife.

"I'm Jessica—Jessica Johnson," she answered quickly. "A friend of Barry Bartowski's. His mom lives here."

The large man's eyes narrowed. "You mean that no-good weasel is back in town?"

"Barry's not here right now. I-I've been helping Celeste." She didn't know what more to say, but suddenly her confusion turned to anger. "Just who are you, anyway?" she demanded hotly.

"Whoa, what'cha gonna do, little lady, throw me out?" His laughter thundered through the house, and Jessica wanted to run and hide. "Don't worry your little head, Jessica Johnson," he added. "We're pretty harmless—at least to our friends." He glanced around the kitchen. "Hey, did you clean up?" She nodded with uncertainty, then he broke into a wide grin that reminded her of a big teddy bear.

"Well, you must be a friend then. I'm Wade, Barry's big brother, and this here's Snake." He pointed to his silent cohort. "How's Ma?" he asked with what seemed sincere concern.

For some reason she decided to trust him. "Oh, she's not too good. I'm worried about her. She needs someone to take care of her. I cleaned and stuff, but she's just so weak—"

"Don't I know it. We just can't find anyone with an ounce of decency. My old lady tries to come over once in a while, but we've been real busy lately. Besides, Ma don't like Joanna much. I hired a gal last week. She worked for half an hour, then stole the TV and left. How long are you and that worm, Barry, going to be in town?"

"I—uh—I don't know." This was all so humiliating. "I'm not really sure where Barry is right now. We got here this afternoon, then he left right away. He didn't tell me—"

"Sounds like the little jerk. Probably off doing a drug

deal or something. You seem like a nice girl, Jessica. How'd you get hooked up with a creep like him anyway?" She looked down.

Wade scratched his beard and shook his head. "I'm gonna check on Ma." He headed down the hall, and Snake slinked off to the living room. Jessica tried not to look at him. He gave her the creeps, and it seemed as if he didn't talk much anyway.

Her cheeks burned in humiliation as she replayed Wade's words about Barry. Could it possibly be true? Not Barry. After all, he'd just scorned his own mother for abusing drugs. Surely he wasn't involved in anything like that. But then she remembered the stuff on his dresser back in Poloma, and suddenly she wasn't sure.

After a while, Wade returned to the kitchen. "Well, Jessica Johnson, you must be good medicine for Ma," he announced. "She looks perkier than I've seen her in weeks. What I can't figure is, how'd that scum, Barry, get hold of you? Ma's worried you might be hungry. We got some leftover pizza in the car. Snake, you go get it!" Wade wrote down a phone number and placed it by the phone. "You call me if you need anything, Jessica. Leave a message with my old lady, Joanna, if I'm gone." He reached out and firmly shook her hand. "Yep, you're all right, Jessica Johnson. Just get away from Barry. I mean it. He's bad news!"

The pizza wasn't bad, and she ate all six pieces. She cleaned and straightened some more and the house slowly became more habitable. It helped pass time, and if she had to stay here, at least she'd be more comfortable. Finally she realized it was past midnight and she was dead tired. Her bag was still in the back of Barry's car so she perused the bedroom she had thought was Wade's for something to sleep in. She quickly realized it was Barry's old room. She discovered an old journal of his, full of poems and songs he'd written in high school—before he'd run away. He sounded so much like her, and once again her heart warmed toward him. Wade must have been wrong about his brother.

But where was Barry now? She dug an old flannel bathrobe out of his closet along with an oversized T-shirt to sleep in. She glanced into the bathroom. After all her scouring and cleaning, she felt desperate for a shower.

As Jessica dried off, she heard Celeste moan from the back bedroom and hurried to see if she was okay. With dripping hair and Barry's robe around her, Jessica peeked in the door.

"Is that you, Jessica?" asked Celeste in a weak voice.

Jessica went in and stood beside her bed. "Yeah, are you all right? Do you want some water or something—I found a couple of tea bags in a drawer."

Celeste coughed. "Sure, some tea would be nice, Jessica, if it's no trouble. You've been so kind already. . . ."

Jessica came back with two steaming cups and sat down. It was almost two A.M. and she felt as if she were walking through a strange dream. She gazed at Celeste and realized how much Barry resembled his mother. Same straight hair, same intense eyes. Celeste must have been a beauty.

"Where's Barry's father?" asked Jessica.

"Sam Bartowski?" Celeste spoke the name with mild irritation. "Somewhere back East, I suppose. He ran off with some blond bimbo when Barry was twelve."

"I'm sorry," Jessica murmured, wishing she hadn't brought it up.

"Good old Sam, for better or for worse. He got the better and gave me the worst. I wasn't sad to see him go, though. I only wished he'd left sooner. . . ." She held her tea with two shaking hands. "I was only eighteen when we got married. My parents had a fit. They had dreams for me. A concert pianist, or at the very least a music degree. But instead I married the high-school football star and had a baby at nineteen. It might've been okay, but Sam knocked me around when times got tough. Times got tough a lot." She coughed, and Jessica was afraid all this talking might wear her out. But Celeste went on. "My nerves were always on edge, so my doctor prescribed Valium. Then I needed sleeping pills. And, yes, Barry told you about all the rest. I knew this stuff would kill me someday, but I just didn't care. . . ."

A lump grew in Jessica's throat. "Do you still feel like that, Celeste? Not caring, I mean?"

"Dying sounds a lot better than this, Jessica. But a little part of me is scared. I didn't used to believe in God. But now I'm not sure. That's what scares me. Because now I know if there is a God, I'm in big trouble. . . ."

Jessica placed a hand on Celeste's bony shoulder. Her memory flooded with things she had heard since childhood. Things like, God was a forgiving God . . . and Jesus died for your sins. "Celeste, I'm certainly not one to tell anyone how to live. I mean, right now my own life is pretty mucked up. But I do remember hearing how God is all about forgiveness and it doesn't matter how bad you've been or what you've done. But if you believe in Jesus and accept His forgiveness, that's about all there is to it."

Celeste smiled a funny smile. "If only it were that simple, dear. Jessica, you look exhausted. Sorry I'm not a better hostess for you. Instead, here you are taking care of me. Thanks for the tea, but you better get yourself to bed. Sleep wherever you like. I know it's horrible, but try to make yourself at home. Did Barry ever come back?" Jessica shook her head and Celeste sighed.

"Good night, Celeste. Call me if you need anything."

7

*J*essica tossed and turned on the lumpy mattress, but she was so exhausted even her own despair couldn't keep her from sleep. She had managed to block most memories of home, but old Zephyr continued to gallop through her thoughts as she drifted into a restless sleep.

"Faster, Zephyr! Faster!" she cried frantically in the hazy reality of her dream. The gray horse streaked through the wheat field and toward a wide ditch. "Jump, Zephyr!" She jabbed her heels into his flanks, only too late. He lunged to one side, and she was flung to the ground at the edge of the ditch. But it was no longer a ditch. Instead it became a deep, wide crevice, and Zephyr was gone now. Stealthy footsteps rustled through the tall wheat and she tried to run, but like two wooden stumps, her legs refused and she sensed her pursuer drawing closer. Suddenly he seized her, and she found herself staring straight into the burning red eyes of something frighteningly wicked—

"Jessica! Wake up!" whispered Barry. "You're having a nightmare, Jessica. Wake up!" She rubbed her eyes and Barry gently shook her. "Are you okay, babe?" His voice sounded concerned, and she fell into his arms, bursting into sobs. He held her and gently stroked her hair.

"I'm so sorry, Jessica," he whispered. "I'm sorry I left without talking to you. I just get so frustrated with this home scene. I went out to get things set up for us to go to New York."

"Really?" She wiped her nose on her shirt-sleeve. "We're going to New York?" She'd dreamed of New York—could it possibly be? "I thought you'd left me, Barry."

"No, Jessica, I couldn't leave you. I love you." He pulled her gently to him and kissed her. She returned his kiss, then pulled away. Her heart had quit pounding now, but she was exhausted and felt incapable of being romantic. But his grip on her arms grew tighter—almost painful, and he continued trying to kiss her.

"Barry, stop it, please. I'm so tired—I don't want this. I need some sleep," she whispered. But he didn't stop. It was almost as if her protests encouraged him, as if he were playing some sick game.

"Barry, I mean it. Knock it off. You're hurting me! If you love me, you'll stop it!" But he continued. Maybe this was her fault. Maybe she'd asked for it by running away with him. But it wasn't supposed to happen like this. She pushed him away again, but he was relentless. His determination made her feel helpless, and for the first time in her life she felt like a victim.

Then suddenly and without warning, something of the old Jessica rared up within her. He had no right to act like this! She clenched her teeth and shoved him hard. He fell to the floor with a loud thud, and she quickly stood, keeping the bed between them.

"Now, you get out of this room, Barry Bartowski! Do you understand?" When she looked down at his angry face, it was like seeing him for the first time.

His eyes narrowed as he stood. No longer the cool, laid-back Barry Bartowski, King of the Coffeehouse, discoursing on world peace and social harmony.

"Jessica," he seethed. "How long do you think you can push me away? If you expect me to take care of you and get you to New York, don't you think I deserve something in return?"

"I don't know!" she whispered angrily. His words confused her. Did she really owe him something? "Look, I don't want anything from you. I'll give you money for this trip. But from here on out I'll take care of myself!"

"Ha! And how will you do that?" He leaped like an animal across the bed and caught her by the arm, jerking her to him. "You *need* me and you know it!" He seized a hunk of her short hair and pulled her head back until she felt her neck might snap. "And even more than that, Jessica—you *want* me!" She doubled her arm, and with all her strength jammed her elbow straight into his stomach. He released her hair. But before she could move away, he smacked her with the back of his fist. Warm, salty blood filled her mouth. That's when she knew without a doubt—she hated him.

"I don't need you anymore!" she screamed. "Now get out of here!" But he continued to approach her with an evil, almost inhuman look on his face. Backing away, she searched for something to use as a weapon, something she could defend herself with, but the room was barren and empty. Her back touched the wall, and Barry drew closer. He looked like he wanted to kill her. Then she noticed a crack of light grow wider behind him.

"You heard her, Barry," Celeste spoke in a low voice. "This is my house, and I want you to leave." But he didn't even flinch, didn't turn around.

"Barry, I'm warning you to get out now, before I call the police."

Finally he turned and glared at his mother, fists coiled. "Go back to your bed, old woman! This is none of your business!"

Celeste clung to the door with one hand for support, and in her other hand trembled a small silver revolver pointed toward her son. She looked frail and weak. One blow from him could have knocked her flat, maybe even kill her. And yet there was fire in her eyes. "I mean it, Barry. Leave at once!"

"This might be your house, but Jessica is mine! And I'll be back for her!" Barry looked into Jessica's eyes with a penetrating gaze of control. Paralyzed with fear, she returned his stare. Could it be true? Did she, in fact, belong to him, even against her will?

She watched until she was certain his car was gone down the street, then she ran around locking all the doors and windows. She checked on Celeste. "I'm so sorry, Celeste. I never should've come—"

"No, dear. I'm the one to be sorry." She coughed for a spell, then caught her breath. There were tears in her eyes. Jessica didn't know if they were from coughing, or from all that had happened.

"I'm sorry I raised such a wicked son," Celeste continued slowly. "And I loved him so much—he was always my favorite. Maybe I spoiled him. As you can see, he only thinks of himself. He has the IQ of a genius, you know. But he just throws it away. I don't understand. . . . He could do anything, and yet he's nothing but a slacker and a dope peddler." Celeste looked down at her trembling hands. Those familiar words reminded Jessica of her brothers' warnings. So they had been right all along. But that didn't change anything for her now. She'd made her foolish choices. She reached for Celeste's hand. This woman may have saved her life tonight, at the expense of her own son.

"Don't blame yourself, Celeste. You know, kids make their own decisions. I mean, look at me, I had this nice family, a big beautiful farm, and I chose to leave." For the first time she actually acknowledged what she had left behind. "And look at you, Celeste. You said yourself you married against your parents' wishes. So you see, you shouldn't blame yourself for Barry's choices. It's not really your fault, not really. . . ."

"Thanks, Jessica," whispered Celeste. She closed her eyes and breathed shallowly.

Jessica stayed by her side until she knew she was asleep.

She tiptoed out and searched for a chair to wedge against her bedroom door. She even found the butcher knife to hide under her pillow. She collapsed on the bed for the second time that night, finally escaping into a dense and dreamless sleep.

When she awoke the little room was full of daylight. Dust particles sparkled in the sunshine above her head. She lay on her back watching them float slowly, moving about like tiny galaxies, participants of a miniature universe. She wondered if that's how God looked upon creation. Was she too just a fleck of dust? Not long ago, she'd been able to talk to God as if He were real and understood her—as if He cared.

It was after ten. She couldn't remember ever sleeping in this late, except maybe when she'd had the chicken pox ten years ago. Maybe she should phone home today. She didn't know what to say, but at least she would call and let them know she was okay—in case they were worried, though she wouldn't blame them if they weren't. But of course, today was Sunday—they would be at church and then out for lunch.

Celeste still slept. Jessica's stomach rumbled, but the cupboards were just as bare as last night. She decided to venture out and hunt down a neighborhood market. She found her purse on the couch, but her money was gone! She clenched her teeth in fury and cursed Barry's name.

"Something wrong, dear?" Celeste asked from the hallway. Jessica looked up with angry tears. Could things get any worse?

"My money's gone," she announced flatly, trying to conceal her rage against this woman's son. "I was going to go to the store for some groceries for us."

"On the top shelf in the coat closet, under those hats and things. There's a black handbag." Jessica fetched the purse and handed it to Celeste. "How much did Barry take, Jessica?"

"I, uh—I don't know. I hadn't really counted it—" Jessica

remembered the cookie jar and wanted to scream. How could she have been so stupid?

"Here, maybe this will help." Celeste handed her a handful of bills.

"Oh, this is too much, Celeste," said Jessica, although it didn't appear to be as much as she'd lost to Barry.

But Celeste clamped her purse shut and shook her head.

"Here're my car keys. I'd greatly appreciate it if you could get us a few groceries, Jessica. For some reason I feel hungry today."

Jessica forced a smile and jotted down a short list and directions to the shopping center.

When she returned, Wade's big motorcycle was parked in the yard and his pitbull tied to the porch again. She avoided the dog and entered through the back door, holding her breath through the stench that permeated the garage. Wade met her in the kitchen and relieved her of one of the bags. He placed it on the counter and sat down beside it.

"So, you're still around, Jess," he remarked, peering into the bag. Jessica remembered how Todd always called her Jess, and her heart twisted. "Ma's asleep right now," Wade continued. "But she told me about the scene last night with Barry. Too bad, but you gotta know by now, he's nothing but a jerk-faced creep anyway."

Jessica nodded. She touched her bruised mouth with her fingertips. It was still sore. "Wade, do you think Celeste would mind if I placed a long-distance call?"

"Nah, you go ahead, Jess. Are you thinking about going home?"

"Well, no. Not really. I mean, I did some pretty bad stuff back home. I wrecked my brother's pickup and broke curfew. I ran away. . . . I even stole money." She looked down at the counter and shook her head in disbelief. Had she, Jessica Johnson, really done those things? It just didn't make sense now.

"Besides," she continued hopelessly. "I'm not really their daughter. I just found out I was adopted. They never even told me before. So why should they care about me?"

"Sounds tough, Jess. But everyone makes mistakes. I'm willing to bet your family still cares." Jessica stared at Wade's Spiderman tattoo and missing front tooth. Who ever would have guessed he was so kind?

"What do you do for a living, Wade?" she asked as she placed some fruit in the refrigerator. She wanted to stall Wade, hungry for someone to talk to.

Wade took a bite from a big yellow apple and wiped his mouth on a grease-imbedded hand. "I run a cycle shop downtown. It's called 'Hog Haven.' Snake works for me. Him and me, and my old lady, Joanna, live in a two-bedroom apartment above the shop." He took another bite. "Yep, it's a great way to live. When the gang decides to take a trip, we just shut down the shop and take to the road. Sometimes we're gone for a month at a time."

"You ride with a motorcycle gang?" asked Jessica. She could imagine it easily. She had seen cycle gangs ride through Poloma before. They'd always seemed kind of frightening with their leather and chains, but Wade didn't scare her.

"Yep, we've got a gang, the Rough Riders. About fifty altogether. But we don't usually all go out at the same time. And we're not your typical biker gang—we have a code. We've got a no-drug rule." He chomped another bite and continued. "See, we've seen too many guys screw up on drugs and take others down with 'em. So a few years back, we agreed on this no-drug rule. Booze is okay, as long as you're sober for the ride."

Jessica shook her head and smiled. She poured a tall glass of milk and ripped open a bag of Oreos.

"That your breakfast, Jess?" asked Wade.

She shrugged her shoulders. "Well, at least for now."

"How 'bout you, Jess?" asked Wade. "You do drugs?"

She laughed. "No way! Are you kidding?"

"Well, I wouldn't know by looking at you. Besides that, hanging out with my idiot brother." Once again, Jessica felt like such a fool. Why had she ever trusted Barry? How could she have ever thought she loved him?

Wade's dog whined from the porch. "I better give Charlie a drink. It's getting pretty hot out there." He filled a big mixing bowl with water.

"Is Charlie dangerous?" Jessica asked, following Wade.

"Depends. Why don't you meet him?" Jessica wasn't sure she wanted to. Charlie hadn't been very friendly so far. But when Wade went out, Charlie wagged his tail, and Jessica timidly patted him on the head.

"Does Celeste have cats?" Jessica asked as she scratched Charlie's ear.

"No, why?" asked Wade, slicking back his greasy black hair.

"Oh, it's just her garage is so smelly, I thought maybe cats might've—"

Wade laughed bitterly. "Oh that! That's from your good friend Barry. Couple years back that dirty skunk decided to make some quick cash by cooking crack—you know, poor man's coke. But when the neighbors started to complain about the horrible smell, he cleared out, and fast. He left Ma to explain it to the cops, and she got stuck with that awful stench. In fact, I just heard how those fumes make people real sick. Sometimes I wonder if that's part of Ma's trouble. Neat guy, that Barry. He talks real pretty and fine, and acts like he's better than everyone, but he's nothin' but a smooth-talkin' hypocrite!"

Jessica didn't know what to say. Suddenly a picture flashed through her mind again. It was Barry's bureau back in his room in Poloma. She knew all those plastic bags and things must have been drug-related, and the suitcase he'd so carefully hidden. How could she have been so deceived?

"I'll try and call home now," she announced. She sat down on the couch and took a deep breath, forcing herself to pick up the phone. Six rings and no answer—

"Hello?" It was Todd's voice. Her heart pounded with panic and she almost hung up, but at the same time felt relieved it was Todd who answered. "Hello?" he repeated. "Jess? Is that you?"

"Yeah, Todd, how'd you know? Don't let on that it's me, okay?"

"It's all right Jess. I'm out in the shop. What are you doing? Where are you? Are you okay?"

"Slow down, Todd. Yes, I'm okay. I'm not really sure what I'm doing. I just wanted to let you guys know I'm all right."

"Jess, come home."

"I can't, Todd."

"You can, and you better! C'mon, Jess, everyone will forgive you. Mom's just sick about this whole thing, and Dad won't speak to anyone. It's like you died or something. Please, Jess, you gotta come home—right away!"

"I just can't, Todd." She started to cry. "Todd, I've screwed up so bad, how can I come back? I mean, you guys . . . you're not . . . you're not even my real family. And I messed up so bad."

"It doesn't matter, Jess."

"It matters to me. Besides Todd, there's something I've got to do. Can you help me?"

"Jess, I don't know. . . ."

The idea had only just occurred to her, but suddenly it seemed the only answer to her problems. "I've got to find out about my real mom, Todd. I can't explain why, but I've just got to. Can you look around and see if you can find an address or something?"

"I don't know, Jess."

"Please, Todd. You've gotta help me. I have to know who she is. Just an address, Todd, so I can write her. I don't think I can ever come home until I straighten this part of my life out."

"I'll see what I can do."

"Thanks, Todd. I know you're not my real brother, but I still feel really close to you."

"Aw, Jess, knock it off with that 'real family' garbage. We *are* your real family, you gotta know that. Are you still with that Barry creep?"

"No, not really. . . . You were right about him, Todd."

"Yeah, I've been doing some talking with Arnie Baker down at the Blue Skye. You know, Jess, Arnie's not such a bad guy after all. He sure doesn't think much of Barry, though. They met in New York. In fact, that's where everyone thinks you are right now. Are you?" Jessica didn't answer and Todd went on. "Anyway, this Arnie guy's all right. I was sort of playing detective, to find out where you might be. Shelly's been helping too. Arnie and I actually had a good chat. He even asked me to do a reading sometime, and I thought I might do some C.S. Lewis. Give those slackers something real to chew on."

"Really, Todd?" Jessica was dumbfounded. Todd reading at the Blue Skye? This was too much. "How come you answered the phone, Todd? Where's Mom and April?"

"Oh, I almost forgot. They think April's in labor, and Mom and Danny took her to the hospital this morning. I guess it's a little early. Might not be the real thing."

"Oh . . ." Jessica felt like such an outsider. "Well, Todd, I'll call back at exactly nine tonight, okay? See if you can find out anything about Susan. Make sure *you* answer the phone, or I'll hang up. Please don't mention my call, okay?"

"Okay, but I really think you should come home right now. Besides, I miss you, Jess."

"Give Zephyr a carrot for me, Todd. Talk to you later." She hung up and felt like part of her heart was being ripped out. How much more could she take? Maybe she should just go back. But she couldn't. She couldn't expect them to just forgive her, especially after all she'd done. She wasn't even their daughter. No, she'd burned her bridges. And she hadn't even told Todd she was sorry about ruining his truck.

Wade left, and the afternoon passed slowly. Jessica hoped desperately that Todd would locate Susan's address. It seemed her last hope. She knew Susan had told them not to tell, but she convinced herself Susan would want her. She'd want to see who Jessica had become. They'd have so much to talk about, so much catching up to do. Susan would understand her. She'd been the same way as a teenager— Dad had said so.

Celeste seemed better and even had an appetite. Jessica kept the doors locked all day, glancing out the window from time to time, pacing back and forth in the kitchen, frightened that Barry might return.

At last nine o'clock came, but when she dialed, the phone just rang and rang. She tried again a few minutes later, but there was still no response. She decided to call tomorrow at the same time. Maybe Todd would remember then.

The next day Jessica played nurse, cook, and housekeeper for Celeste again. It helped pass the time. More than that, Celeste needed her, and it was sort of nice to be needed. Jessica thought if Todd couldn't find anything out about Susan maybe she should stay and help Celeste. Thankfully, Barry hadn't come back. She discovered her bag stashed in the garage—another one of his tricks. But at least now she had a few clothes to wear. Occasionally she caught her reflection in the mirror. She loathed her hair and her clothes. They were just another sickening reminder of her stupidity.

"Do you have any family, Celeste?" Jessica asked as she laid the dinner tray on the bedside table. "I mean, any brothers, sisters, parents—you know." Celeste seemed weaker tonight, and Jessica wondered if there was anyone besides Wade to help out. Wade, with his heart of gold, just didn't seem to understand the amount of care his mother required. He acted like she was going to get better and everything would soon be okay. And he still hadn't had any luck finding a caregiver.

"No, not really. I was an only child. My mother died just last year." She sighed. "And I haven't spoken to my father since I left home." Her eyes had a faraway look, almost a longing. "I went to the funeral, and my father wouldn't even speak to me. And of course, I didn't try to say anything to him."

"Does he know about how sick—"

"I really don't think he'd give a hill of beans about what happens to me." She leaned back and looked up. Jessica followed her gaze up to the smoke-yellowed ceiling. She wanted to say something, some words of comfort, but her mind was completely blank.

"Well, try to eat something, Celeste. You need to keep up your strength." Celeste attempted a feeble laugh, and Jessica closed the door behind her. She leaned against the wall and took a deep breath. Caring for Celeste was becoming oppressive. As much as she'd grown to love this woman, she knew she couldn't continue on like this. She felt like she was suffocating. It was as if someone had placed a bag of rocks on her chest.

Wade's cycle roared into the yard, and Jessica ran eagerly to open the door. She looked forward to his visits. They helped break the monotony of her days.

"Hi, Jess, how's it going? Is Ma any better?"

"I don't think so, Wade. In fact, she seems weaker to me." Jessica didn't like relating bad news, but she was worried about Celeste. "Is there anything that can be done for her?"

"I don't know. I just keep hoping she'll lick this and get a second chance."

"I know, Wade, but what if that's not the case? What if she's really dying? Don't you think her dad should be informed—"

"That old coot . . . forget it! He was never anything to her. Or us. Grandma wasn't half bad—at least she came around some. She and Ma got along okay. But that old codger was too good for everyone. Kind of like my little brother, which figures, since he was named after him."

"Well, I don't know, Wade. When I mentioned her father to Celeste, it almost seemed like her eyes looked hopeful—just for a second. I thought maybe if he came . . . well, it might perk her up. You never know."

"Really?" Wade scratched his head. "You know, I'd do anything to help Ma. But I just don't think he cares. But if you really think it'd do any good, I'll give the old man a call. Guess the worst that could happen is he could hang up."

"Thanks, Wade. You never know, people can change. . . ."

"I suppose miracles can still happen," he said cynically. He went into the kitchen and looked in the fridge. "Guess who I saw in town today, Jess?" He popped open a soda.

She knew by his voice. But she didn't want to answer. It still hurt to think about Barry. Her memory played tricks on her. Sometimes she could only recall the things she had been attracted to—his sensitive eyes, his ideals, and how good his arms felt around her. Then it was like two different people when the ugly truth hit her and she remembered who he really was. She despised herself for falling for his lies.

"Well, anyway, I warned little brother to keep away from you," Wade announced with pride. "And he knows I mean it too. I don't think he'll be bothering you anymore."

"Thanks, Wade. I hope so."

Wade went in to see his mother, and Jessica wandered out to the tiny backyard. It was still hot out, but at least the air was fresher than the stuffy house. She only felt safe being outside when Wade was around. The grass was parched and brown. A dilapidated picnic table sat on a tiny, cracked cement slab that she supposed was once a patio. Had their family ever had a barbecue here? Had they ever sat around that table and laughed and eaten and enjoyed one another? She doubted it. Old tires and other pieces of junk lay cluttered about the yard. The only trace of life was a climbing rosebush on the east fence. Actually, it was planted in the neighbor's yard, but a wayward vine had crept through a broken picket in the fence. She wondered why it didn't creep right back.

Then Jessica remembered Mom's lush vegetable garden bordered by flowers, and how her prize rosebushes lined the drive. She mentally compared their acreage of fruitful cultivation to this stubby little square of dead grass. Life just didn't make sense, and she was getting tired of trying to figure it out. Maybe if she could meet Susan, her real mother, the puzzle pieces would finally fit. Maybe life would start to make sense again. She wondered what Susan looked like. Would she have dark heavy curls like Jessica used to have? Now that she thought about it, Jessica realized she didn't resemble anyone in the family she'd grown up in. Funny she'd never considered the possibility before.

At exactly nine she called home again. On the second ring Todd answered, and she sighed in relief.

"Todd, thank goodness you remembered!"

"Sorry about last night, Jess," he said in a hushed voice. "But April had her baby! Everyone was so excited, and I forgot all about your call. I went to the hospital with Greg to see her. It's a girl—Amanda Jane Johnson, and pretty cute too—for a baby, that is. Mom's so happy, she's almost back to her old self. . . ."

Jessica felt glad for them, but she felt something else. She felt replaced. Maybe this little Amanda Jane, a true Johnson, would have Jessica's room. April had been complaining about how hard it would be for her and Greg to share their room with a baby. Maybe Amanda would grow up on the farm and ride Zephyr. She could be Grandpa's girl. Jessica knew it was silly, but she felt jealousy over the birthright of an innocent baby.

"Jess, you still there?"

"Yeah, Todd. That's great news." She tried to sound enthusiastic. "Did you have any luck getting the address?"

"Sure did. I mentioned to Mom today that maybe we should write Susan and let her know about what happened. Sort of like warn her that you know now, and everything. Mom actually gave me the address, but I don't really want to write. You got a pencil? Here it is: Susan Miller, 67845 Villa Court, Seattle, Washington. There isn't a phone number. Are you going to write her?"

"Maybe. . . . Thanks Todd, I really appreciate it. Go ahead and tell the folks I called, and that I'm okay. By the way, I'm in New York, and I love it here. I'm working in a coffeehouse, and I plan to stay—"

"But, Jess!"

"Thanks for everything. Goodbye, Todd."

"Wait—"

She hung up. She had to, before she broke down. Lying to Todd was one of the hardest things she'd done. But her family ties were broken now, completely severed. She could be replaced by Amanda, and rightly so. Hopefully, Amanda Jane would turn out better than Jessica. Hopefully, Amanda Jane wouldn't bring shame to the Johnson name the way she had. If she could go back in time, she would. She would reverse all her wrong choices that had led her down this crooked road. But even that would never alter the fact that she wasn't really one of them.

8

*J*essica plunged the breakfast dishes into the hot, soapy water. Another day. How long could she go on caring for Celeste, and consequently fearing Barry's return? She had to figure a way out, a way to get to Susan. But she knew she wouldn't abandon Celeste. The doorbell dispersed these thoughts and a soapy juice glass escaped her hands and shattered on the floor. She tiptoed barefoot past the broken shards, praying not to find Barry on the front step. Instead, there was an elderly gentleman in a crisp white sport jacket. He looked harmless so she cracked open the door.

"Does Celeste Bartowski live here?" he asked politely, with an air of formality. Instantly, she knew he was Barry's grandfather and opened the door wider.

"I'm Barry Rothwell," he said, clearing his throat. "And I've come to see my daughter Celeste." He looked nervous.

"How do you do, Mr. Rothwell. I'm Jessica. I'm a—a family friend." She showed him in, suddenly feeling conspicuous and self-conscious. "Celeste is in bed. I'll see if she's awake. You do understand she's very ill?" She searched his face for any sign of emotion or sympathy. He nodded solemnly with a trace of sadness in his dark eyes. Maybe he did still care.

"Celeste, your father's here to see you," whispered Jessica.

Celeste's white skin paled even more. "Here? In this

house? Whatever for?" She clutched her sheet with wide eyes.

Jessica nodded and tried to smile. She hoped this wasn't a big mistake. She clasped Celeste's hand. "Don't worry, Celeste. He seems like a nice man. Should I bring him in? I'll stay close by. . . ."

Celeste straightened her bedspread and smoothed her hair. "All right, Jessica. I guess so," she whispered.

Jessica led him in. He gasped when he saw his daughter, then stood frozen at the foot of her bed for what felt like a very long time. At last he went to her bedside and actually knelt down on the grubby carpet. He began to sob.

"My poor little Celeste, what an old fool I've been—"

Jessica swallowed the lump in her throat and quietly closed the door. She knew she should be happy for them, but somehow all she felt was a sense of futile hopelessness. She went to the kitchen and swept up the broken glass, then finished the dishes.

She stared blankly out the window across the tiny parched yard. The green of the wandering vine caught her eye once again, only this time there on a slender stem rested a small pinkish blur. She placed the last plate in the drainer and went outside.

The perfect rosebud with its succulent petals stood out in stark contrast against the dry splintered wood of the rag-gedy fence. She carefully picked the blossom, leaving plenty of stem, and inhaled its sweet perfume. How could some-thing this lovely exist in this barren desert of a yard? Of course, she knew its roots were nurtured next door, where some faithful gardener watered and fertilized. But for some reason, this brave, wandering rosebud seemed like a miracle to her, as if it contained some secret message that she couldn't quite decipher. But she felt certain it had come from God.

She placed the tender stem in a tumbler of water and set

it on Celeste's lunch tray. Just then the front door flew open and she turned in surprise.

"Barry! What are you doing here?" she stammered.

"I came for you, Jessica. Ready to go to New York?" he asked brightly, as if nothing had ever come between them.

"Barry, I'm not going to New York with you. Or anywhere else for that matter." She tried to keep her voice calm.

"Oh, sure you are. Come on, get your stuff." He caught her roughly by the arm. "Let's get going, Jessica. I'm in a hurry."

"I'm not going with you, Barry. Let go of my arm right now!" But his grip tightened and he jerked her toward the back door.

"Just a minute, young man," announced the senior Barry from the hallway. Celeste lingered just behind him, a faint shadow leaning on the wall for support. "The young lady has made it perfectly clear she's not going with you."

"This is none of your business, old man!" snarled Barry. "You were nothing to me as a kid. What makes you think you can walk in and tell me what to do now?"

"I told you she's not going. Now, leave her alone!" Barry's grandfather said with convincing authority. "I mean it, Barry. We don't want trouble. You just be on your way now, and everything will be okay."

"Fine!" Barry exclaimed, releasing Jessica with a shove. "But I'll be back, Jessica! You'll see!" He slammed the door behind him, and Jessica sighed in relief.

"I'm sorry—" Celeste faltered, crumbling to the floor. Together, they gathered her up and carried her back to the bedroom. Her breathing was uneven and labored, but she slowly regained consciousness. Mr. Rothwell watched as Jessica gave her some sips of water, but Jessica noticed the lines of worry crease his forehead as he clasped and unclasped his hands.

Later, Mr. Rothwell inquired about Celeste's care situation.

"Well, I happened to stop here with Barry, which I know now was a mistake—Barry, I mean. This place was in a horrible mess. Celeste really needed some help, so I pitched in," Jessica explained. "I really like her, but I don't know how long I can stay and take care of her. And she certainly can't survive on her own."

"I understand," he said. "Celeste told me about how you got here. It's none of my business, but I think you should get as far away from Barry as possible. And the sooner the better. I plan to assume full responsibility for Celeste from now on. I'll take her to my place and hire a nurse to care for her. I discussed it with Wade. I've already wasted so much time with my foolish pride. God only knows how much she's got left. I didn't know she was so bad off. If only I'd known sooner . . ." He buried his head in his hands.

Jessica was dumbfounded. In such a short time, she'd come to feel Celeste was her personal responsibility. Now suddenly it seemed to be over.

"Oh, that'll be so good for Celeste," she exclaimed. "And for you too, Mr. Rothwell. I really care about Celeste, but I need to sort out my own life right now."

"I understand. You've done a lot for her, Jessica. How can I thank you? Do you need money?"

Jessica looked down. She knew she did, but her pride kept her from admitting it. "No, Celeste gave me some." Unfortunately, it wasn't enough to get her to Seattle.

"Well, you just tell me if you need anything. I plan on moving her to my house this very afternoon. I'll hire an ambulance to transport her."

Jessica nodded, relieved for Celeste's sake. But at the same time she felt dismissed. Celeste had needed her before, and it gave Jessica an odd feeling of security. Now that she was free, she didn't quite know what to do.

The familiar roar of Wade's motorcycle sounded in front. Jessica wondered what he thought about all this. But when he entered the room, he shook hands with his grandfather. She knew some kind of truce had transpired between them.

"So, Jess, what'cha gonna do now?" asked Wade.

"I think I'll head for Seattle. My mother lives there, and I want to pay her a visit."

"Hey, you need a ride? The gang's all heading for the Northwest tomorrow. I've decided not to go. I want to stay close to Ma for now. At least until she gets stronger. But Snake and my old lady, Joanna, are going. You could probably ride with Joanna."

Jessica had never been on a motorcycle. "You mean it?"

"Sure. They're going up through Colorado, over the Rockies, and on up to Portland, Oregon. You'll have to get a bus or something from there. But it ought to be a great trip, and you'll be in good hands with Joanna."

Wade called his wife, and they quickly worked out the details. It was decided that Jessica should spend the night with Celeste and her father, just in case Barry returned. She and Wade spent the rest of the morning packing things for Celeste and getting the house ready to close up. Celeste insisted she didn't need an ambulance, but Mr. Rothwell wouldn't have it any other way. Jessica rode with Celeste. It gave her an eerie feeling to ride in the silent ambulance. Celeste lay on the stretcher, white as a ghost while the attendant watched her carefully.

The Rothwell home was a rambling estate, built in the southwest style with golden stucco and surrounded by beautiful terraces and gardens. Jessica marveled that Celeste had exchanged all this for the sad life she'd chosen. But that, supposedly, was love. In the enormous living room stood a grand piano next to a window-filled wall. Jessica watched the hunger in Celeste's eyes as the attendant guided her wheelchair past the dark, gleaming instrument. Would she finally be able to play it again?

The maid helped situate Celeste in a lovely room, with French doors that led out to a terra-cotta patio surrounded by gardens. A fountain bubbled into a small pond nearby, and a hospital bed had already been set up and adjusted so Celeste could easily see out the window.

"Oh, Celeste, isn't it beautiful!" gushed Jessica. She plumped the fluffy pillows up behind Celeste.

"Yes, I'd almost forgotten," breathed Celeste in wonder. "This used to be the best guest suite. You had to be important to stay in this room." A tear slid down her cheek and she clutched Jessica's hand. "Thanks, Jessica. I know you had a hand in this."

"Is it hard coming home after all these years?" Jessica asked.

"Not exactly hard. Just painfully wonderful." Celeste leaned her head back, sighed, and closed her eyes.

"Get some rest, Celeste."

Jessica crept from the room, unsure of what to do next. She longed to explore this amazing house but didn't want to wear out her welcome. She still marveled that Celeste could have turned her back on all this for the likes of someone like Barry's father. But of course Celeste was young back then, and—well, Jessica understood.

She sat down on a white leather couch in the front room and picked up a glossy travel magazine. Absently, she thumbed through it. She felt awkward and out of place here. Although she wouldn't mind staying, she knew she didn't belong.

"There you are, Jessica," Mr. Rothwell said. "Now, you make yourself at home. I just spoke to an employment agency, and they'll be sending out nurse applicants first thing tomorrow. Is Celeste settled in okay? I'm sorry I was tied up when you arrived."

"That's all right. The maid showed us in. Celeste is asleep now."

"Good—good. I want her to be perfectly comfortable. I've contacted my own doctor about a specialist for her and already made an appointment for a complete exam." He stood and stared off into space for a few moments, then back at Jessica.

She nodded dumbly. There didn't seem to be much to say. She gazed down at her black dress. She knew it looked weird, but it was the only thing she had that was clean. She wished she'd brought some normal clothes from home. But Mr. Rothwell didn't seem to notice. He smiled at her and reminded her to make herself at home, then excused himself.

She decided to hunt down the laundry facilities. After an interesting search, she located a large, well-equipped laundry.

"What are you doing in here?" exclaimed Gina, the maid. "I'm supposed to do the laundry. You're the guest!"

Jessica laughed. "I'm sorry, Gina. I'm used to doing my own laundry. Do you mind?"

"Okay, just don't let Mr. Rothwell find out. Is this all you have?"

"Yes. I left in sort of a hurry. I had to pack light."

Gina shook her head. "Doesn't look like much."

Jessica's face grew red as Gina left. Gina probably had more clothes than she had, plus Gina had a job, even if it was being a maid. Jessica separated her lights and darks to create two micro-sized loads, then perched on the big counter with a magazine to wait for her clothes to wash. Wouldn't Mom love this laundry room? It was so big and efficient. There were racks to hang clothes on in a small drying room—even counters and sinks. All this for one man? She thought of Mom's laundry area on the back porch. Too hot in summer, too cold in winter, and always full of baskets bulging with grimy clothes. Life was funny.

After her laundry was finished, she checked on Celeste. She found her propped in bed, with a stack of magazines and a big glass of iced tea, complete with lemon wedge.

"Come sit, Jessica," Celeste invited. "I was afraid I might not see you before you left. When are you going?"

"Tomorrow, early. Joanna's supposed to pick me up. I hope she doesn't mind. What's she like anyway? Do you know her?"

"Well, Joanna's different. We didn't always get along. But she's nice in her own way. And you can trust her."

Jessica glanced out the window and saw a couple of birds splash in the fountain's spray. "This is such a beautiful place, Celeste. You should be happy here. I've never seen anything quite like this, except maybe in movies. And your father has contacted some special doctors for you."

"I know, I can't believe it. It's like a dream after all these years. I almost feel like a little girl again. It's good to be home." Celeste had a coughing spell, and Jessica knew she should let her rest.

"I'll come back later tonight to tell you goodbye. You keep resting, Celeste. It's been a busy day for you."

Jessica ate a late dinner with Mr. Rothwell in the big dining room. It felt awkward and strange, but she imagined she was a character in a movie. Someone else. Each new day she felt parts of Jessica Victoria Johnson disappearing, simply vanishing.

"More coffee?" asked Gina, interrupting Jessica's thoughts.

"Sure, thanks," she replied.

"Well, Celeste seems to be resting well," Mr. Rothwell commented. "I think she'll be comfortable here."

"Oh, it'll be so good for her, and her room is so nice. It's a shame she couldn't have come sooner—" Jessica wanted to retract her words when she saw the hurt on Mr. Rothwell's face.

"I know, I know. . . . If only I hadn't been so stupid and stubborn."

"What do you mean?" asked Jessica.

"Oh, years ago when Celeste ran off with that Bartowski—I was so angry. My own little girl throwing her life away like that! In my mind, I pretended she'd died. I think I actually believed it. It was easier that way. My dear wife, Constance, tried to keep in touch with Celeste. But it was always behind my back. Because if I found out, I'd make it difficult for her. The funny thing was, after a while I was sorry. I even wanted Celeste back in my life, but I didn't know how to go about it. Pride, I guess. Try as I might, I just couldn't bring myself to go to her. I always thought one day she'd come to me. I was just waiting. Then last year, after my wife died, I thought she'd come back. I didn't realize she was so ill. . . ."

Jessica didn't know what to say. She stared at the frozen peach dessert still on her plate.

"I'm sorry. I shouldn't burden you with the meanderings of a foolish old man." He wiped his mouth on a linen napkin.

"No, I don't mind."

"Ready for your adventure tomorrow? Are you certain you're up for this? If it's the money, I'd gladly give you plane fare, just as a token of thanks for all you've done—"

"Oh, no. I think it'll be fun." This was partly true. She did think it might be fun, but the thought of flying to Seattle was very tempting. Yet her pride kept her from accepting his offer.

"Well, you young kids. I guess I just don't understand. . . . By the way, Gina mentioned you might be a little short on clothes. I know it's none of my business, but I thought I'd mention—well, my wife was about your size, tall and slender. . . . I haven't been able to bring myself to clean out her closets yet. Maybe you could find some things there that you could use."

Jessica was embarrassed. It was such a sweet and sincere offer, how could she refuse? But to wear the clothes from an old dead lady, she shuddered. "Well, I guess I could look."

He smiled and led her and Gina back through another wing of the house. She hadn't been this way yet. They entered a spacious master suite, and he showed her a huge walk-in closet, as big as her bedroom at home. She expected to find pastel polyester pantsuits, but instead she was surprised to find some really nice clothes. Nothing like an old grandma's closet.

Gina smiled knowingly. "I told Mr. Rothwell I could get anything you liked all laundered and ready for your trip tomorrow, Jessica."

"Oh, thank you. That'd be great."

"Constance liked to shop. She always kept up with the latest styles—very fashionable. People thought she was younger than her age. It was such a shock when she died. . . ."

"I'm so sorry. But if I judged her by this closet, I'd guess she must've been a very interesting lady."

Mr. Rothwell smiled. "That's right. Now you go ahead—take anything you like. I think Constance would be happy to know you could use them. Especially after all you did for her daughter. This will help me. I've been planning for some time to have Gina help me go through these and get them sent out to the Salvation Army. You're doing me a favor by getting us started."

She selected a pair of khaki pants and some jeans, a couple of nice shirts, and a brand new denim jacket with the tags still on. A pair of Keds fit perfectly.

"This is great, Mr. Rothwell. Thank you so much!"

"Thank *you*, Jessica. Are you sure you don't want more?"

"No, I better keep it light. But thanks anyway."

She decided the clothes were perfectly clean and told Gina not to worry, then carried the treasures back to her room. Gina had given her the room next to Celeste's, not so large, but just as elegant, and it overlooked the same pretty garden. She peeked into Celeste's room. It was late, but she wanted to say goodbye.

"Come in, Jessica," said Celeste softly. "Turn on the light. I want to talk to you."

Jessica sat in a white wicker chair next to the bed. "I wanted to tell you goodbye, Celeste. You know I'll be leaving in the morning."

Celeste nodded. "Are you going to be okay, Jessica? I mean, I feel kind of responsible for you. I have a feeling if my son hadn't come into your life, you'd still be a happy girl, back on the farm with a family who really does love you."

Jessica swallowed the lump in her throat. "I don't know, Celeste. Sometimes I think our destiny is all planned and charted out before us. Maybe we just play these parts as they're given. . . ."

Celeste leaned back and closed her eyes. "I used to believe something like that, but I'm not so sure now. It's funny, I've been thinking about what you said about God and forgiveness the other night. It reminded me of some things my own mother used to say. I'm beginning to think we make our own choices in life, but God's just waiting for us to turn to Him to help us out of our messes."

"Hmm, maybe. But then sometimes our messes can take us places we still need to go. Like if I hadn't gotten hooked up with Barry, I never would've met you, Celeste. And I might never have found out about my real mom. You know, I don't even hate Barry anymore. Somehow getting to know you and your father has helped."

"You've been through a lot, Jessica. But I want you to listen to the advice of a woman who already learned the hard way." Celeste reached for Jessica's hand and looked into her eyes. "I know your parents love you. I can tell by you, Jessica. You are a fine girl who made some bad choices, probably due to Barry's influence. Don't forget, you can always go home. I just know it—" She began to cough and Jessica gave her a glass of water.

"I've worn you out, Celeste. Don't try to talk anymore. I'll remember what you said, and I'll write and tell you how it goes in Seattle."

Celeste nodded with tears in her eyes. Jessica knew they weren't just from coughing. She gently hugged Celeste's frail body.

"Thanks for everything, Jessica," breathed Celeste. "I still think you're an angel sent from God."

Jessica laughed uncomfortably. "God must've been pretty desperate. I'll always remember you, Celeste."

Jessica left the room and burst into tears. She knew it was the last time she would see Celeste. Despite Wade and Mr. Rothwell's hope, she knew Celeste would probably not live much longer. That thought hurt deep inside. It was like nothing she had ever felt before. She was only three when Grandpa Johnson died, and she barely remembered him. But Celeste was different—it almost felt like Celeste had grown to be a part of her. But she wasn't sure why or how. She packed her backpack and dropped the little black dress in the garbage, along with some of the other things she could no longer stand to look at. She was finished with that part of her life. She saw herself in the mirror and realized that awful hair would continue to remind her of what she had thrown away. Her face was pale and drawn now. She knew she'd lost weight. She was no longer that robust Kansas farm girl ready to pose for the milk commercial. Only now she didn't care.

9

$\mathcal{G}$ina tapped lightly on the door just as Jessica pulled on her jeans. "Joanna's here, Jessica."

"I'm coming—thanks, Gina." Jessica shoved her feet into her new shoes from Celeste's mother and grabbed her bag. She glanced into Celeste's open door. All was peaceful and quiet. Jessica's heart whispered a wordless prayer; she knew she wouldn't see Celeste again.

Outside, the big shiny Harley looked out of place in front of Mr. Rothwell's manicured drive. A woman about Jessica's height but twice as hefty leaned against the big black bike. She wore tight black leather, and her hair was the color of straw. She looked tough. Suddenly Jessica was unsure.

"Hi, Jess!" she called. "I'm Joanna. You'll ride with me. Have you ever been on a Hog before?"

"Huh?" asked Jessica.

"You know, a Harley—a Hog, a bike. Ever ridden?" Joanna pointed to the bike and looked at Jessica like she was demented.

"Uh—no, but I'm sure I'll get the hang of it."

"Sure, nothing to it. Just follow my lead and hold on tight. This all you got?" asked Joanna as she reached for Jessica's pack. She nodded.

"That's good. I was worried you might've packed the kitchen sink." Joanna gave a few pointers and they were off. Jessica held on tight, not exactly afraid, but the sight of hard asphalt speeding below made her uneasy. They continued on out of town and stopped at a rest stop where dozens of other bikers were waiting.

"Yo, Jo!" Snake called from across the lot. "How's the ride, Jess?"

She looked at him in amusement. It was the first time she had ever heard him speak. "Pretty good. I think I'm getting the hang of it."

"She's doing fine, Snake. We might make a biker of her yet." Joanna laughed. She slapped Jessica on the back and greeted friends with names like Zipper, Granny, Doctor Doo, and the Vet. Jessica wondered if she'd keep them straight. Everyone seemed to respect Joanna. And to Jessica's surprise, Joanna appeared to be calling the shots.

They rode north on the back roads and passed through Wichita Falls before noon. Jessica wondered how far they were from Wichita, Kansas, though it seemed a lifetime away. Waves of homesickness swept over her at the familiarity of grain farms and wide-open spaces, but the wind dried her tears before they even touched her cheeks. They stopped in a little town for chili dogs, and Jessica offered Joanna money for gas.

"No way, Jess. Wade gave me strict orders. You save your money. You'll probably need it."

Jessica swigged the last of her Coke and placed the empty bottle on the old red soda machine. She felt someone watching and turned to see Zipper—at least that's what she thought his name was. He swiped back his straggly blond hair and smiled in a sleazy sort of way. His beady eyes traveled up and down. She walked away in disgust, glad to join Joanna.

This time Jessica relaxed a little on the back of Joanna's cycle. Her death-hold grasp loosened and she began to enjoy the ride, the scenery, the freedom, and the wind in her face. She trusted Joanna's ability to safely guide the powerful bike along the highway.

They crossed into New Mexico around six. Jessica was tired, thirsty, and hungry. She'd emptied her water bottle almost two hours earlier. But soon they pulled into a state park situated on a lovely turquoise blue lake, with tall trees bordering. She'd always pictured New Mexico as a desert state and now was pleasantly surprised by the natural beauty.

It was still hot so they decided to take a swim before setting up camp. They all laughed and played in the cool water, but every time Zipper came near, a chill traveled down Jessica's spine. Something about his pale blue eyes and that sly grin made her skin crawl. She thought about mentioning it to Joanna but didn't want to sound like a baby.

"Can I help, Joanna?" Jessica offered back at camp. "We used to camp a lot. I bet I can pitch this tent."

"Great, go ahead." Joanna unpacked her bike, and Jessica was amazed at how many supplies fit into the compartments.

"Wow, Joanna, looks like you've got this down to a science," Jessica said with admiration as Joanna set up a nifty little campsite.

"You bet! Wade and I've been doing this for years, but I decided some time back we could do it a lot easier. Now I carry a full line of compact camping accessories at the bike shop. I've even thought about making a little booklet, you know. To show other bikers how they can do it too."

"Joanna, you really should! You might even make money."

Joanna laughed. "Now, wouldn't that be something."

Snake and Doctor Doo joined them for a hearty dinner of spaghetti and meatballs.

"How'd you guys get your names?" asked Jessica.

"Oh, it's pretty simple," Doctor Doo said. "Take me.

My real name is Leroy Doolittle—thus Doctor Doo."

Jessica nodded. Doctor Doo seemed like a nice guy, probably in his forties, but he just didn't look like a biker. "You're not really a doctor are you?" she asked.

He laughed. "No, just a C.P.A. But Wade and I go way back. In fact, I knew Wade's mom, Celeste, in high school."

Jessica stared into the fire. She hoped Celeste was okay.

Snake rolled up his T-shirt sleeve and exposed a tattoo of a fierce king cobra. "This is how I got my name, Jess," he said.

She glanced at his skinny bicep and nodded. "Uh-huh, I see. . . . Joanna, how come you and Wade don't have names?"

"Wade does. They call him Fang, because of his tooth, you know. That's why he won't get it fixed. And, well, I'm just Jo, and that's fine with me."

"I'll do the dishes, Jo—since you cooked." Jessica gathered the tin plates and things and headed for the pump on the edge of camp. It was dark, but her eyes slowly adjusted as she squatted by the pump and scrubbed. Just as she was rinsing the last greasy pot, a pair of dusty boots sauntered up. She looked up to see Zipper hovering over her with his thumbs hanging on his belt loops.

"Need some help, Jess?" he asked in a whiny voice with a strong Texas twang.

"Nah, thanks—I've got it." She stacked the clean dishes and stood, recklessly dumping the rinse water right on his feet. She smiled inwardly as it splashed on his boots, then took a step back.

But he moved closer and breathed right into her face. "Just trying to be friendly, Jess." His breath stunk of beer, and she turned to escape, but before she could, he ran his hand down her back. She stopped and clenched her teeth. She could smack him, but instead she stormed back to camp. The sound of his laughter echoed through the trees and filled her with rage.

She sat next to Joanna by the dying campfire and fumed silently. She wouldn't mention Zipper. Not yet. She jabbed the embers with a stick and watched the sparks fly up to the sky.

"You know, Jess," said Joanna, "what you did for Celeste was real nice. Wade appreciates it a lot. Sorry about Barry, though, but I guess it's best you found out what a jerk he is. Though I still can't figure how a girl like you got mixed up with the likes of him. Guess it just shows, you can't judge a book by its cover."

Jessica nodded and studied Joanna's face, softened by the firelight. She realized Joanna was one of those books too. "How'd you meet Wade, Jo?"

"Oh, let's see, it's been so long. . . . We met in high school. Wade had a Hog back then. But it wasn't that cool to be a biker. Though no one made fun of Wade. No one dared. He was big then, too. I was just this nobody. A mouse, a zero. A skinny, zitty, dishwater blonde. My folks were poor, and I worked at a greasy spoon to help out. Then Wade came in one day and recognized me from school. I couldn't believe it—I mean *nobody* knew me. And he'd come in every once in a while and was always real nice, always tipped. Before long we became friends."

Jessica couldn't imagine Joanna as a nobody. Joanna, in her own way, was so self-assured, so in control. "What happened then?" Jessica asked with impatient curiosity.

"Oh, I'd daydream about becoming a biker chick," Joanna continued. "I'd dream about wearing leather and bleaching my hair, and riding with Wade. But he never seemed too interested in me like that. No, we'd just talk and talk, but he never asked me out. Still, he didn't really have another girlfriend either. Sure, he'd bring in girls sometimes and I tried not to be jealous. It wasn't hard, 'cause he never

treated them like they were anything special. But his friend-
ship helped me, and pretty soon I started feeling better
about myself. He treated me like I mattered. He even encouraged me to go to business college after high school, and
I did. In fact, I even worked for Doctor Doo awhile. Then
this other C.P.A. started asking me out and I figured Wade
and me were just friends, so I went. Wade threw a fit and
we've been together ever since. We got married on our Har-
leys."

"Oh, Jo, that is such a romantic story!"

Joanna laughed. "You think so? Well, Wade's all right."

———————

Jessica slept soundly next to Joanna in the tent.

The next morning, Jessica started to dismantle the tent.

"Hey, what'cha doin'?" Joanna asked. "We're not leaving until tomorrow, Jess."

"Oh, okay, I didn't know." Jessica sighed in relief; her
seat was still sore from the previous day's long ride. She
stuck close to Joanna, and they hiked around the lake in the
morning. After lunch they found a nice little beach and
lazed about, taking dips in the lake when it got too hot.

"What a way to live," Jessica commented as they
stretched out on the sand. "If only life were always this simple and free . . ."

"Yep, but it's not. So you just gotta make time for these
moments and take them when you can." Joanna rolled over
on her stomach, and Jessica studied the tattoo on her left
shoulder. It was just like Wade's, only hers was Spider-
woman."

"Did it hurt to get that tattoo?"

"Uh-huh."

"Why'd you get it?"

"Oh, it was pretty dumb. I kinda wish I hadn't. But it
was the thing to do a few years back. All the biker chicks

were getting 'em to prove how much they loved their men. This one gal, Cindy Lou, made a big stinkin' deal, 'if I really loved Wade,' you know. So I did. Really stupid! I mean Wade never even liked it and it took longer and cost more than all the other gals'. Funny thing is, Cindy Lou ditched her man just a few weeks after." Joanna laughed. It was a big, hearty laugh that seemed to go right up to the tops of the trees.

Later that evening they all rode into town for dinner. The townsfolk stared and gave them a wide berth. Jessica wanted to giggle, but it would spoil the tough exterior the bikers were so famous for, with their leather and chains and shocking tattoos. The people's fear gave her an odd sense of power. She wondered if the other bikers felt it too.

After dinner they lingered in the parking lot, joking and horsing around. Some were ready to party and others were heading back for camp.

"Hey, Jo, Jess can come with me," announced Zipper, swaggering over to Jessica's side.

She looked desperately at Joanna, begging her with her eyes to intervene. But Joanna just stood with her hands on her hips and said nothing.

"C'mon, Jess. I'll show you a good time." He grabbed her by the hand.

"I don't think so," Jessica faltered, not wishing to make a scene. She pulled away, but his bony grip remained firm.

"Aw c'mon, Jess. I don't bite. At least not usually." He laughed in a vulgar way. By now several other bikers looked on. Jessica wished someone would step in, but they all just watched in silence. Suddenly she felt like an outsider. Maybe they didn't really care. After all, Zipper was one of them; she wasn't. Zipper pulled her toward him and grinned. "Yeah, Jess, I bet you like to dance."

"Get your hands off me," she said loudly, standing her

ground. Joanna stepped up beside her, almost like a backup. But still she remained silent.

"Hey, that's what I like, a feisty woman!" Jessica tried to pull away, but still he didn't let go.

"I said, get your slimy hands off me!" she yelled. The others stepped up.

"You heard her, Zipper," said Snake. "The lady doesn't like your style."

But Zipper ignored him and pulled her closer.

"I just think she's playin' hard to get," he sneered.

Jessica for once appreciated Snake, but why didn't anyone else say anything? She clenched her fists in anger. Then Joanna nodded slightly at Jessica and smiled. Jessica tried to jerk her hand free once more, then in final desperation cut loose with her other hand and smacked Zipper right across the face with her fist. He released her and grabbed his bleeding nose. She stepped back and watched in horror as the bright red liquid oozed between his fingers. The crowd applauded.

"Okay—okay, I catch your drift," he muttered as he stumbled away.

"Good thing for you, Zipper, because next time you'll answer to me!" announced Joanna with authority. She turned and headed for her bike, and Jessica followed with rubbery knees. Now she understood. Joanna had wanted her to stand her own ground. Jessica didn't want to hit anyone, but maybe it was the only language someone like Zipper understood.

The next day they rose at dawn, ate breakfast, and started to break camp. It was routine now; Jessica knew what to do and made herself useful. She didn't want to burden Joanna.

"Jessica," began Joanna, unwrapping a parcel. "I don't know if you're interested or not, but I thought you might like these." She unfolded a pair of dark brown leather pants and a matching jacket. Jessica felt the soft grain of the leather, obviously not new, but very nice. She looked at Joanna in wonder.

"But, Jo, where'd you get these? Are you sure?" Jessica could tell they looked to be about the right size.

Joanna nodded. "It was Wade's idea to give 'em to you at first. He got them for me years ago, back when I was still skinny." Joanna held them up and shook her head in disbelief. "Anyway, I told Wade I'd get to know you, and if you measured up to everything he said you were . . . well, here." She handed them to Jessica and smiled.

"Oh, Joanna, this is really great. I don't know how to thank you—"

"Well you can start by putting them on. I want to see if they fit."

Jessica climbed out of the tent and turned around in front of Joanna. "They fit!" she exclaimed.

Joanna smiled. "Makes me happy to see them back in use, Jess. I know you'll do 'em proud."

They traveled in the cool of the morning. The leather made Jessica feel like a real biker, plus they kept her warm. The landscape was spectacular in the mountains, and they followed the Rio Grande River up into Colorado. Jessica had never seen anything like the majestic Rockies, towering to heights she'd never imagined. She longed for a camera and tried to indelibly print the scenery into her mind. They stopped in the Rio Grande National Forest and camped by a mountain stream. Jessica liked the soft crunch of tree needles under foot and the pungent smell of the pine resin warmed by the afternoon sun. After making camp, she and Joanna stretched out in the shade by the rushing stream. The sound of gurgling water seemed timeless and almost ethereal. Jessica gazed at the branches overhead, framing the deep blue sky. There had to be a God. How could a world this beautiful simply evolve? Still she wondered what

God might have in mind for her. Could He really forgive a girl who had broken all the rules?

The next few days they traveled the winding, breathtaking roads north through the Rockies. Jessica didn't worry about the hairpin curves or sheer drop-offs below. Instead, she focused on the enormous rocky cliffs. They looked as if they'd been hand-chiseled by some gargantuan hammer. Sometimes the beauty was almost too painful to enjoy, because in comparison her own life appeared ugly and small. They passed through Wyoming and Idaho, camping in beautiful unspoiled spots, hidden like gemstones on seldom-traveled roads. Jessica trusted Joanna and told her all about her problems. About Barry. About finding out she was adopted. Joanna listened quietly, and without judging.

Finally, they followed the Oregon Trail along the Columbia River until they arrived in Portland, their parting place. The bikers would tour on down the Pacific Coast Highway, stopping here and there along the coast. Jessica almost wished she could continue on with them. Instead, she stood before the old brick train station with a lump in her throat. "Joanna, how can I ever thank you? You've been like a sister."

Joanna hugged her tight. "That's all the thanks I need, Jess. Now, you keep in touch, ya hear? Stay out of trouble and take care." Jessica watched as Joanna roared out of the parking lot. An older couple shook their heads in open disgust, whispering, Jessica was certain, about how there ought to be a law against rowdy motorcycle gangs. She threw back her head and laughed.

The next train to Seattle wouldn't leave until six, so Jessica searched out the rest room. She longed for a shower but instead made herself at home in the ladies' room. She washed off the road dust, then shampooed her hair in the little sink and dried it under the blow dryer on the wall. She studied herself in the mirror. Dark roots were already be-

ginning to show where her hair had grown out. She was almost used to it now. And now she knew the real Jessica was
more than hair and clothes. Identity couldn't be purchased.

She wondered what her mother, Susan Miller, would
look like. But she didn't allow herself to think about what
Susan's reaction to her might be. No, that was too scary to
consider. She would cross that bridge later.

With a few hours to kill, she got a stale hero sandwich
from a kiosk that had everything from diapers to tobacco
pipes. She took it outside and sat in the shade. Soon, an elderly woman pushing a shopping cart loaded with rags and
bags plodded up beside her and sat down on the bench,
breathing heavily. She wore a faded pink polyester dress
over dark brown trousers that were worn and stained and
frayed around the bottoms. Her dirty feet seemed to ooze
out of a pair of bright neon surfer thongs. The woman
stared at Jessica's sandwich.

"Want some?" asked Jessica, holding out the sandwich.

"*Danke*—thank you. Bless you, child," the woman said
in a thick accent. She grabbed the sandwich and devoured
it. Jessica had half a cup of coffee left that tasted like an old
boot, but she offered it to the woman, who eagerly accepted.

"I have not eaten for days," said the woman, though her
round figure belied her words. "Mein name iss Freida, and
who might you be?"

"Jessie."

"Jessie, das gut name. Iss short for Jessica?"

Jessica nodded. "Where are you from, Frieda?"

"Ach, you mean mein homeland? Iss Deutschland, ya
Germany. I come to dis country in 1946. After zee war, you
know? Ya, I vas only fifteen." Freida pulled a faded and torn
table cloth from her cart and wrapped it around her shoulders.

"Do you have a home, Frieda?"

"Oh ya, ya. I have mein home—a beautiful home. Up

there." She pointed to the sky and smiled. "Ya, dat home iss vaiting for me. Got is goot, you know. You must believe Him—and His son Jesus Christ. Dat iss de only vay to de kingdom, you know. . . . Dat iss de only vay to home. You have home?" Frieda looked at her. Jessica wasn't sure which Frieda meant. In fact, she wasn't sure of either answer.

"Uh, yeah, I guess so. . . ."

"Not goot, Jessica. You must know vhere your home iss. Or else you got no home."

Jessica decided to change the subject. "Do you have a family, Frieda?"

Frieda looked to the sky again and nodded. "Ya, and soon I go see mein family. Mein sister, and Mama and Papa. Soon ve'll be together."

"What about children . . . any family around here?" Jessica was getting concerned about Frieda—was there anyone who might care for her?

Frieda rolled up a pink sleeve and showed Jessica a tattooed number on her arm. Jessica shook her head as a shock wave ran through her. She'd heard about Nazi prison camps but had never actually met a refugee. "Ya, I vas in Dachau, along vith mein family. Mein little sister, not strong like me. Mein mama and papa too old. Only I live. In Dachau, the doctor, he do many things to me."

Jessica shuddered. "Oh, Frieda, I'm so sorry. How awful."

"Ya, iss awful—must never forget. But mein hope iss heaven—a new life for me." Frieda slipped off into a German song. Jessica tried to make out the words and figured it must be a hymn. Her harsh voice couldn't carry a tune, but the sincerity in Frieda's soft brown eyes gave meaning to the music beyond words and melody. Something stirred in Jessica as she looked into Frieda's careworn yet peaceful face. It was almost as if she'd glimpsed God. Then Frieda stood and removed her tablecloth. She carefully folded it and handed it to Jessica.

"Thank you, Frieda." Jessica reached for her purse. She knew this woman wasn't begging, but Jessica had to give her something. She pressed a ten-dollar bill into her hand. "Here, I hope this'll help tide you by, Frieda."

"Danke, danke. Thank you, Jessica." Frieda pushed her cart and lumbered off, singing tunelessly as she went.

10

*J*essica sat next to the window on the train. She knew it wouldn't arrive in Seattle until late, and a wave of worry washed over her as she wondered what she would do. Where would she stay? And for the first time since leaving home, she felt completely alone and cut off.

It was her first train ride. She leaned back into the seat and allowed the soothing motion of the train sink into her. Across the aisle, a mother rocked her crying baby, and a small girl kicked her feet loudly against the seat and asked again and again if she could get a drink.

Finally, Jessica offered to take the little girl. The weary mother looked at her hard, and then back to the girl who continued to whine. The mother nodded. Jessica took her by the hand and walked back to the fountain next to the bathroom. The girl barely took a sip and was finished. Jessica took her right back to her mom, and the woman smiled in relief.

"Thank you," she whispered. "I think the baby's asleep now. We've been on this train since noon and I'm exhausted." She carefully laid the baby beside her, wedged between an overstuffed diaper bag and the back of the seat.

"He's sweet," Jessica whispered. The sleeping baby had his thumb in his mouth.

"Thanks," said the woman. "They always look sweet when they're sleeping."

"I'm going up to the diner. Would you like me to bring

you anything?" Jessica offered.

"Can I go, can I go?" begged the little girl. Jessica smiled and looked at the mother.

"Do you mind?" the woman asked. "I don't want to impose. . . ."

"No problem." She took the girl's hand. "My name's Jessie, what's yours?"

"Shawna, and my mom's name is Karen." Karen stuck some money in Shawna's hand and told her to bring her back a sandwich and a soda.

They found a sticky table in the diner, and Jessica ordered a French dip. Shawna had a burger and an Orange Crush, then ordered the same for Karen—to go. She seemed very adult for a young child, and nothing like the monster who had been kicking the seat and whining.

"So Shawna, how old are you?"

"Almost seven," she answered with her mouth full. "But I'm Mommy's 'second hand,' 'cause we don't got no daddy. So I get to help her a lot." She wiped ketchup across her sleeve before Jessica could suggest a napkin. "Yep, we been on this train all day. We're going to Tacoma to see my grandpa. We're gonna stay for a whole week. We used to have a daddy, but he left. Mommy said he wanted to live someplace else. But I don't see why he didn't take us—we could live someplace else, too. I'd even give my cat away if Daddy's place don't let cats in. My grandpa's place don't let cats in. I had to leave my cat home, but that's okay 'cause Molly Ann's gonna watch him. My cat's name is Bart." They finished eating and took Karen her burger and drink.

"Thanks, Jessie," said Karen. "I hope she didn't talk your leg off." Jessica laughed and visited with Shawna a little more while Karen ate her dinner. Then she went to the back of the car and sat alone.

It was odd, during this whole crazy trip, she'd seldom allowed herself to be alone with her thoughts. In some ways it was a relief, because her thoughts were so confused. She watched the countryside flash by the window—rolling hills covered with tall evergreen trees. So different from Kansas. She allowed herself to remember the farm, her family. Rather her adopted family. They were probably worn out after a hard day's work. She couldn't believe it had been only two weeks since she'd run away and not quite a month since she first met Barry. It seemed like another lifetime. She could imagine Todd stretched out across the living room floor, all six feet three inches. She pictured Mom cleaning up the dinner dishes in the kitchen. April was probably busier than ever with the new baby. Would anyone miss Jessica?

She'd tried to cover her trail, only mailing a postcard as she left a place. She hadn't sent anything since Wyoming. It probably didn't matter. It didn't appear anyone was trying to stop her anyway. Well, at least they knew she was alive. Maybe Zephyr missed her. Was this what the saying 'burning your bridges' was all about?

Barry came to mind. He was the one person she hadn't allowed herself to think of. Her face still burned with humiliation when she realized how she had fallen for his smooth lies. How could she have been so foolish? Would she ever make the same mistake again? She remembered how Dad used to say "it's one thing to make a mistake once, but only a fool repeats it."

What was ahead for her? Would she meet her real mother? How odd, for the first time in her life to actually lay eyes on a blood relative. And why did it matter so much anyway? These answerless questions tormented her, and the wheels on the track seemed to echo her thoughts, saying, '*what-lies-ahead—what-lies-ahead?*' over and over until she thought her head might explode. She pulled down a pillow from the overhead rack and wrapped it around her ears to muffle the taunting sound and soon dozed off.

"Next stop, Seattle," was announced over the loud-speaker. Jessica rubbed her eyes and looked around the dimly lit car. She reached under the seat for her bag and pulled it to her lap. Her backpack was stained and dirty. She remembered when it was new; Dad had brought it home for her to use for volleyball. Their team had almost gone to state last year. Now that life seemed so far away. Unreachable. Outside, the city lights glimmered. Seattle looked huge; she hadn't imagined it to be so large. She still had no idea what she'd do for the night. It was after eleven. She couldn't just pop in on Susan unannounced at this time of night.

She counted her money, still plenty for a night in a motel. She had never stayed alone in one before. In fact, she'd only been in a motel a couple of times, once with her family in Wichita and last year at a high school yearbook convention. Sadly, she remembered Poloma High. She'd been chosen to be assistant-editor of next year's school paper, *The Poloma Press*. Now it was all behind her. Even if she could go back, what would they think of a girl who had run away with a dope peddler?

"Everyone out for Seattle. The next departure will be delayed twenty minutes. Thank you for riding the *Pioneer*." Jessica scooped up her bag and climbed off the train.

She wandered down the nearly deserted terminal and considered spending the night in the train station and finding something in the morning. Some guys were hanging out by the bathrooms. She'd never actually seen a gang, but they looked suspiciously like one to her. She approached an information desk just as the woman flipped over the closed sign.

"Excuse me," Jessica said.

"Sorry, I'm off duty." The small, dark-haired woman's eyes looked tired, and Jessica turned away. "Okay, just a' quick question then," said the woman kindly.

"Oh, thanks. I just need to know where a decent motel .

that's close by might be. But not too spendy."

"Well, there's a Motel Nine within walking distance, but you shouldn't walk around here after dark." The woman eyed Jessica and sighed. "I suppose I could drop you off, if you want."

Jessica couldn't believe her luck. She thanked the woman profusely as they walked through the parking lot. Then she noticed a faded sticker on the bumper of the woman's VW Rabbit: "Smile, God loves you." Jessica grinned and climbed in.

The motel wasn't much, but at least they had a vacancy. The tiny room smelled of stale cigarette smoke, but the shower felt wonderful, especially since it was the first one she'd had since Texas. She unfolded the khaki pants and white shirt from Barry's deceased grandmother and draped them in the bathroom, hoping the steam would remove some of the creases. She still felt funny about wearing a dead woman's clothes, but tomorrow she wanted to make a decent impression. She stared at her hair in the mirror and wanted to scream, the wind and sun had turned it into what looked like a wild haystack. She pulled a comb through and wondered how long it would take to grow.

The next morning she awoke early, carefully dressed, and checked out of the motel. The desk clerk told her where to catch the bus to take her to the city center. On the bus, she observed the neatly dressed business people. Everyone looked like they had done this a million times and would do it a million more. No one noticed her. No one knew she would probably meet her mother today for the first time. She got off on a busy street and was greeted by the hiss of brakes, horns honking, and the smell of diesel exhaust. Tall buildings towered above, banks and offices, and some huge department stores. Wouldn't Shelly be impressed? She stood on the corner and took it all in. Everyone else bustled along, hurrying somewhere. She wondered where they all were going. What did they all do here in the city?

Then, to her surprise and delight, she spotted a familiar sight. A set of Golden Arches wedged between two tall buildings. She hurried over and joined the long line of business people. They seemed unlikely customers, and yet there they were waiting, like her, for their Egg McMuffins. The man ahead of her wore a three-piece pinstriped suit and read a *Wall Street Journal* as he waited. She picked up her order and found an empty seat in the corner, then ate slowly. She was in no hurry. She watched as others popped in and out. They steadily came and went, rubbing elbows with strangers without talking or even smiling. Just hurrying off on their busy way. Such a strange life.

Back on the street, she noticed a girl about her age emerge from what looked like a beauty salon. This girl's hair was cut in a shoulder-length bob and looked shiny and neat. Jessica touched her hair. It felt like straw. She wondered if they could do anything with it. The shop looked pretty busy, but the receptionist said she could fit her in right then if Jessica was ready.

"Hi, I'm Cherise. What can I do for you?" asked an attractive black woman. Jessica sat down in the vinyl-upholstered chair and stared at her reflection in the mirror. It was like a stranger was looking back at her. A stranger with a very sad face.

"Well, about three weeks ago I had my hair bleached, and now I hate it. Is there any way to get it back to its normal shade?"

Cherise fingered Jessica's hair. "Well, honey, it's in pretty bad shape. If I put more chemicals on it, it might all fall out."

"Oh," Jessica sighed sadly.

"But I could give it a conditioning treatment, and then if you still want me to try, you'd have to sign a release form. It might work okay, though. Your hair is still nice and thick."

"Okay," agreed Jessica. "I'm desperate!"

Cherise looked at her strangely. "Well, honey, I can't work miracles." Jessica told Cherise about why she had bleached her hair in the first place and about how she was meeting her real mother today. Cherise nodded and listened with empathy.

When Cherise finished, Jessica couldn't believe it—her hair was back to it's natural color.

"Cherise, it's wonderful. Thank you so much. It even looks shiny and healthy."

"You're one lucky girl. But you should buy some of this conditioner to keep it looking good."

Jessica took her advice and paid the cashier. On her way out, she noticed an elderly woman leave a tip for the beautician. Jessica did likewise for Cherise, and thanked her again. Cherise was wrong. She *was* a miracle-worker.

"Well, you just take care, honey. And good luck with your mother."

Jessica counted out the money that Celeste had given her to replace what Barry had stolen. It had dwindled fast. Would it even be enough to pay for a taxi to her mother's house? And what then? It was almost ten o'clock. She wondered if her mother would even be home. In the city, it seemed like everyone worked; possibly Susan did too. And suddenly Jessica was plagued with doubts. What if her mother didn't really live here? What would she do? She was almost out of money in a strange town where she knew no one.

Jessica sat down on a bench by the bus stop and stared into the busy street. Her eyes couldn't focus on the traffic, and her head swam. She missed Kansas, missed home. She wondered if the new baby was sleeping in her room. Did the family miss her? Or were they glad she was gone? After all, Dad had said she was just like Susan, and he seemed glad that she had left. She thought of the money she had taken.

And how she had run away, sending only a couple of post-cards to let them know she was alive. It seemed her old life was gone and dead. The familiar lump grew in her throat and she wiped a tear from her cheek. She would not succumb to self-pity. She'd made her bed, as Dad would say, and now she'd have to sleep in it.

A bright yellow cab drove slowly by and she waved at it, just like she'd seen in movies. Surprisingly, it stopped. She showed the driver the address and explained she was low on money.

"Well, then, if I was you, I'd take bus 54 on over to Sinclair and then catch a cab from there—save you some dough." She thanked him and took his advice. The next cab driver wasn't as congenial, but at least he deposited her in front of the right address. She paid him and climbed out.

Jessica felt conspicuous in the nice upper-scale neighborhood. The homes were set back and apart and seemed to be carved into the gently sloped hills. They were traditionally styled, each with carefully landscaped yards. Even the dark green plastic trash cans that lined the street matched.

She slowly walked up the shrub-lined path to the front door of a white house trimmed with black. Her mind was blank and her mouth was dry. She didn't even know if she could remember her own name. She took a deep breath, pushed the doorbell, and stood dumbly on the porch with no idea of what she would say. A little boy of about five opened the door. He stood before her in an oversized white T-shirt with skinny bare legs poking out beneath. He was holding a piece of toast thickly coated with purple jam that matched the smears on his shirt.

"Hi," he said brightly. "Who are you?"

"My name is Jessie. Does Susan Miller live here?" she asked politely, her heart pounding.

"You mean my mommy?" He caught a glob of jam on

his tongue just before it dripped to the slate floor under his feet.

"Yes, is she home?"

"Jerred," a voice called from within. "Is someone at the door? Don't answer it."

Jerred grinned. "I'm not s'posed to answer the door when Mommy's in bed. Did you come in that yellow car? Where'd it go?" He peered out the front door.

"Yeah, it's gone. It was a taxi." Jessica took a breath, trying to compose her nerves. "Can you tell your mommy someone wants to see her?"

"Ya wanna come inside?" asked Jerred. Obviously his mother's warning meant nothing to him. He grabbed her hand with sticky fingers. "C'mon, I'll show you my fish. His name is Oscar—you know like on Sesame Street."

"Well, Jerred, I better wait out here—"

"Jerred Anthony Miller! I told you not to answer the door!" scolded a woman in a pale blue bathrobe. Jessica stared in amazement. She knew she was seeing her mother for the first time. "What is it?" Susan demanded. "What do you need? You better not be selling something, because solicitors aren't allowed in this neighborhood."

Jessica's mouth was like paper. She tried not to stare, and she was afraid she might cry. "I uh . . . I came to see Susan Miller."

"Oh, are you from the nanny agency?" asked Susan, her voice warming some. "You look sort of young. Do you have much experience? The agency is supposed to call before they send someone—"

"I like her, Mommy," interrupted Jerred. "Can we keep her? She's lots nicer than those other old ladies." A loud wail interrupted them.

"That's Ashley, my baby," explained Susan, then disappeared down the hall. She came back with Ashley in her arms. "Jerred, you take her to the family room for me."

Jerred led Jessica by the hand to a large, sunny room just off the kitchen. Jessica grabbed a paper towel on her way and wiped the sticky jam off her hand.

"You have a baby sister?" asked Jessica as she sat on the sofa. She reached beneath her to remove a toy jet.

"Hey, I was looking for that!" Jerred zoomed it around the room, jumping over toys strewn across the floor. "Yeah, Ashley is my sister, but I hate her. I wanted Mommy to take her back. We don't need no stupid crybaby."

Jessica grinned and looked around the room. It was nicely furnished, but it appeared this family needed a maid as badly as a nanny. She wondered what Susan would say. She didn't seem very friendly. What if she wanted her to leave? Jessica toyed momentarily with the idea of pretending to be from the agency but decided to play it straight. Lies only caused problems in the long run.

"So, how old are you?" asked Susan. She carried the fussing baby into the kitchen and placed a bottle of formula in the microwave. Jessica walked over and pulled out an oak barstool and watched her with fascination. This was actually her mother! She was pretty, but her face looked sort of tight with frown lines in the middle of her forehead.

"Actually, I'm sixteen and a half," Jessica began as she sat down. She was careful not to place her elbows on the jam-streaked counter.

Susan turned to her in surprise. "Well, that just won't do. I need a nanny year-round, not just for the summer. I won't waste any more of your time. The nanny agency should've told you."

"I'm not from the nanny agency." Jessica looked straight at her, wondering if Susan might guess. There *was* a similarity between them.

The microwave beeped, and Susan removed the bottle and tested the milk on her wrist. She stuck it into Ashley's mouth and turned to Jessica. "Well, who sent you, then?

How did you know I needed a nanny?" Susan sat down in the rocker in the family room, her attention focused on quieting the fussy baby.

Jessica studied this strange, yet familiar woman. She made a pretty picture, almost something you might see in a greeting card. A pretty mother holding her baby, sunlight streaming in all around. She was small and thin. Her hair was lighter than Jessica's, but it curled softly around her face. Susan looked up at Jessica with a puzzled expression, almost as if she were annoyed that this strange girl was still here. As if Jessica should have quietly let herself out and disappeared. Instead Jessica evenly returned her gaze and instantly recognized her own gray eyes in her mother's face.

"I'm Jessica Johnson, from Poloma, Kansas."

The color slowly drained from Susan's face, but she said nothing, just stared in shock. The baby contentedly drank her bottle with loud sucking noises.

"Mommy!" called Jerred. "Come help me!"

Jessica looked at Susan and the contented baby. "Want me to go?" she offered. Susan nodded blankly and Jessica took off, following Jerred's cries down the long, dim hallway. She found him sitting on the toilet with his big shirt hiked around his middle, little legs dangling.

"Help me," he demanded. Jessica rolled her eyes, pulled out several yards of toilet paper, and told herself this was really no worse than shoveling manure.

"You know, Jerred, you're old enough to do this yourself," she mumbled in disgust as she flushed the toilet. He ran off giggling, and she slowly washed her hands and stared into the mirror. What now?

"What do you want?" asked Susan from the doorway in an angry whisper. The baby was almost asleep in her arms. "What did you come here for?"

"I just wanted to meet you. . . ."

"Well, you've met me." Susan turned and went down the

hall. Jessica followed, lingering at the door of a pink-and-white baby's room. Susan carefully laid the sleeping baby in a pretty white crib and tiptoed from the room.

"Jerred, for Pete's sake, go get dressed!" exclaimed Susan as they returned to the family room.

"You're not dressed, Mommy," argued the five-year-old as he stomped off.

"Jessica, I don't understand this. Betty and Dan were never supposed to tell you about me. That was part of our deal."

Jessica looked down, remembering that awful night. "They didn't exactly tell me. . . . I overheard and I demanded to know. They couldn't help it. And Todd's the one who found your address for me."

Susan sank into the couch and stared into space. "Little Todd? He was just a baby last time I saw him. Sweet baby, too. And Danny Jr. I guess was about Jerred's age, with Greg somewhere between. I remember when I realized I was pregnant, I was tempted to keep my baby, just because Todd was so cute. But my mom sent me to Wichita, to keep my secret. It was funny, fate I guess, because Betty was pregnant too. Not quite as far along as me." Susan stood up and walked over to pour a cup of coffee.

Jessica didn't want to say anything, didn't want to break the spell, as Susan continued almost as if in a daze.

"Yes, Betty got pregnant a couple months after I did. Little Todd was still in diapers, but Betty didn't mind. She was certain it would be the little girl she'd always wanted. But she had some sort of complications. I never knew exactly what because I was in Wichita then. Betty ended up in Wichita, too, right after Christmas. Poloma's tiny hospital had no prenatal unit back then; they probably still don't. Such a tiny little town. Betty lost her baby and almost died herself. She had to stay in the hospital for a couple of weeks. Strangely enough, I went into labor while Betty was still there. I'd already planned to give up my baby, but no arrangements had been made. Suddenly it seemed so fitting for Betty and Dan to adopt my baby. Because after Betty lost hers, Dan said she couldn't have any more. They were thrilled, but I made them promise to never contact me and I would never contact them."

"Why?" asked Jessica.

"Well . . ." Susan ran her fingers through her hair and took a long sip of coffee. "I knew what it felt like not to fit in. When my mom got divorced, we had to live with relatives. They didn't want me. Then Mom married Dan's dad and we moved to Poloma. I didn't fit in there either and I wasn't really a Johnson and . . . well, I just didn't want that for *my* baby—I mean you—" She stared at Jessica in wonder. "I didn't want that for you. And besides, Betty and Dan were the nicest people I knew."

Jessica appreciated that.

"But now you pose a problem for me, Jessica. My husband, David, doesn't know I ever had a baby. And I don't want him to know. He wouldn't understand. He was brought up in this completely normal, traditional kind of family. I told him I was orphaned as a young child. So you see, you'll have to leave."

Jessica was stunned. Just like that she was being dismissed. After all she had been through just to get here. "But I wanted to get to know you," she began. The tears were burning in her eyes. Susan hadn't even wanted to know anything about her. Didn't she even care?

"I'm sorry. But you really should've called before you came. In fact, I'm surprised Dan and Betty even let you come all alone like this."

"Varoom!" yelled Jerred as he flew his jet through the family room. He tripped over the rug and landed smack into Jessica's lap.

"Better watch out there, Commander Jerred," warned

Jessica with a shaky voice, still trying to hold back the tears. He looked up and smiled brightly.

"Wanna come see Oscar now?" He tugged on her arm, and she followed. Anything to escape the mother who didn't want her.

"See, that's Oscar," Jerred announced proudly. He stood with his face plastered to a fish tank where only one extra-large goldfish swam about contentedly. The goldfish had brownish spots. "I call him Oscar 'cause he's always dirty," explained Jerred. "You know, like Oscar in the trash can on Sesame Street."

Jerred showed Jessica his room and talked her into reading a book about airplanes to him. She didn't mind; it helped delay the inevitable. She read the lines of the book, wondering where she should go, what she should do. She envied Jerred. He had a room of his own and someone to care for him. Of course, he was too little to understand or appreciate what it all meant. She wished she could turn back the clock, change her choices, and be back in her own room again. Like in *The Wizard of Oz*, Jessica looked down at the Keds from Barry's grandmother. If only she could click her heels together three times and go back to Kansas too.

11

*J*erred followed Jessica to the family room like a miniature shadow. She wondered if somehow he sensed something. After all, he was her half brother. She picked up her bag and headed for the door.

"Hey, wait, Jessie!" yelled Jerred. "Where ya going? I want you to stay!" He grabbed tightly to her leg. "Read me another story."

"What's going on?" Susan demanded, now dressed in faded jeans and a T-shirt. "Jerred, let go of her leg—right now!"

"No, she's gonna leave. I want her to stay. Jessie can be my nanny—I like her better than those grumpy ol' grannies. I want her to stay!" Jerred started to cry, and Jessica was afraid she might cry too.

"Hmm," Susan mumbled, scratching her head. "I suppose you could be our nanny for a little while, Jessica. I mean, if you're interested. . . ."

Jessica stared at Susan. "What do you mean?"

"Come with me," Susan instructed. "Jerred, you go play. Mommy needs to talk to Jessie alone." Jerred slid his arms off Jessica's leg and looked dubiously at his mom, but he obeyed. Jessica followed Susan to the den.

"We just might be able to pull this off, Jessica," Susan said confidentially as she closed the door behind them. She sat behind a large oak desk. "Are you willing to play along?"

"What do you mean? You want me to be your nanny?"

"Yes. I'm having a hard time finding someone suitable. I want to return to work as soon as possible. This full-time mom thing's getting to me. Jerred seems to like you. What do you think? Want to try it for a while? That way you can stay and 'get to know me better' as you say. The catch is, no one must know you're my daughter. Understand?"

Jessica nodded. She didn't like deception, but on the other hand she had no real alternatives. And this way she'd be around her mother. Besides, in time Susan might grow to care for her. Maybe she'd invite her to stay indefinitely. Maybe they would become close.

"Okay," Jessica said slowly. "What do I need to do?"

"First, you must pretend to be eighteen and have lots of baby-sitting experience. Fortunately you look older. I guess we'll have to keep your name, since Jerred already knows it. It shouldn't matter anyway, because David's never even heard of a Jessica Johnson." Susan went on to detail the job responsibilities and then showed Jessica to a tiny room off the garage.

"This will be your room. We'll rig up the intercom from the baby's room so you can hear Ashley in the night. I'll start back to work next week. Thankfully, that means no more late-night feedings for me."

"Where do you work?" asked Jessica.

"I'm a legal secretary for my husband's firm—Miller, Simpson, and Jones. David keeps saying he doesn't want me to go back to work, but I can't just vegetate around here for the rest of my life."

Jessica nodded like she understood, but she didn't. She couldn't figure how a woman would willingly leave her children in the hands of a virtual stranger. Especially if she didn't have to. Susan was bubbling, though. Her face seemed to light up with the prospect of having a nanny and returning to work. Jessica hoped it also had something to do with having her long-lost daughter here, but she wasn't sure.

Susan showed Jessica how to care for Ashley and where

things were. Thankfully, Jessica did have some baby-sitting experience from working in the church nursery. Everyone had always said she got along well with kids. She kept hoping Susan would take a break, that they could sit down together and really talk. Jessica wanted to tell her all about what had happened in her life the past few weeks. She longed for Susan to listen and understand. Instead, Susan took her over a long list of everything that had to be done, going from room to room. Jerred trailed them everywhere and clung to Jessica like a long-lost buddy.

"Jessie, why don't you try this out for the afternoon? That way I can get some shopping done," Susan suggested. Jessica felt unsure but didn't want to disappoint Susan. She agreed to give it a try. Maybe this was a test. Maybe if she proved she could pass it, Susan would accept her and everything would be fine.

Jessica managed to fix lunch and care for the baby, as well as play with Jerred. By midafternoon, she got them both down for naps and didn't know what to do. She decided to straighten the kitchen and family room; Susan had pointed out that it was part of the "job." She was tired but didn't really mind the work. It was such a nice home, and really not that difficult to clean. She imagined Susan coming back, smiling and thanking her.

"Hello? Anyone home?" a man's voice called from the garage entrance. Jessica jumped in surprise. That must be David. What would he think of a stranger in his house?

"Hello, Mr. Miller," said Jessica, stepping into view. "I'm Jessica, the new nanny." She held out her hand in greeting.

He stared at her. "Where's Susan?" he demanded.

"Well, she uh—she went shopping," Jessica stammered.

"Just great!" he exclaimed. "I leave my wife home with the children and come home to some strange teenybopper in her place!"

Jessica glanced at her watch. "Susan should be back soon—"

"Daddy!" exclaimed Jerred as he dashed down the hallway and flew into his father's arms. David swooped him up, tossed him over his shoulder, then carried the giggling bundle into the family room and dumped him on the leather couch.

"How's my man?" asked David, and Jerred attacked him all over again.

Jessica heard Ashley's cries and slipped out to check her. She changed her and warmed a bottle, then carried her back to her little pink room, hoping to avoid David. He seemed pretty grumpy. Jessica cradled Ashley in the rocker and fed her. She had done this in the church nursery, but it still felt strange. She quietly sang the song she used to love as a little girl, ". . . Blacks and bays, dapples and grays, all the pretty little ponies . . ." The song reminded her of her own gray pony back on the farm. Suddenly she felt someone's eyes upon her and stopped singing. David stood in the doorway with a puzzled expression. She looked away in embarrassment, and he left.

A little later, Susan came home and threw together a makeshift dinner. Jessica was invited to join them and helped set the table. She carefully folded the napkins and laid the silver straight. If only she could get them to like her.

"Well, I'm so excited about returning to work," said Susan as she passed a carton of store-bought potato salad. "I swear, it's made me a new woman." David scowled, but Susan continued on without noticing. "I found this perfect outfit at Greyson's, it's so classy. I can't wait for Monday. I'm so glad today's Friday. It's funny, I used to be thankful for Fridays because of the weekend. But now I'm thankful because it means I get to go work sooner."

Jerred, who was seated next to Jessica, picked at his food. She tried to encourage him to eat. Tried to act like a nanny. "This tastes yucky!" he yelled. "I wanna hot dog!"

"Jerred, mind your manners," said David. Jessica heard Ashley fussing and left to check. She picked up the baby, thankful to be away from them. But their conversation still drifted down the hall.

"I told you not to get a nanny, Susan!" David said in anger.

"Well, I did, and I'm glad! I'm certainly not going to rot my life away in this house just because I have kids!" yelled Susan.

"I wanna hot dog!" hollered Jerred.

"Shut up!" shouted Susan.

"Don't talk to him like that," David scolded her. "Maybe you're right. Maybe we do need a nanny. Then maybe, for a change, these kids would be cared for properly."

"See?" shrieked Susan. "You never appreciate me! I slave away taking care of your kids all day, then you waltz in and accuse me of being a terrible mother!"

"I wanna hot dog!" screamed Jerred at the top of his lungs. A door slammed, then another. Jessica peeked out and tiptoed down the hall with Ashley in her arms. Only Jerred remained at the dining table and he was sobbing.

"It's okay, honey," soothed Jessica. She stroked his golden curls and wiped potato salad from his face.

"I-I just wanna hot dog," he sobbed pathetically. Jessica made a hot dog for him, balancing Ashley on one hip while she did. Ashley patted Jessica's face and laughed.

She sat Ashley in the high chair and fed her strained carrots the way Susan had told her to. She studied Jerred's tear-streaked face as he poked down his hot dog. Was this all her fault? Had she brought disunity to this home? Maybe if she worked really hard, she could make things easier for everyone. Maybe she could make them happy, but if not she would leave.

Jessica put a Mickey Mouse video in for Jerred and laid Ashley on a baby quilt with some toys. Occasionally she heard someone stir at the other end of the house and figured it must be Susan.

As the night progressed, she wondered when to put Jerred to bed. Susan hadn't said anything about bedtime. Ashley seemed content to play and Jerred didn't look too tired.

"When do you usually go to bed, Jerred?" asked Jessica. He didn't answer. The movie ended, and Jessica turned off the TV.

"No—another one! I want Donald Duck!" he demanded.

"If you want to watch another movie, then you can ask nicely and say 'please.'" Jessica smiled at him, and he looked down sheepishly at his bare toes. She stood before him, arms folded, waiting.

"Okay, Jessica. Please, I wanna watch Donald Duck," he said quietly.

"Bravo!" said David from the hallway. His face was transformed from the angry man she had met earlier. He walked in and sat on the couch. "I'm sorry I sounded so put-out at you, Jessica. It's not your fault; you just got caught in the middle of a family squabble. Actually, I'm pleased with how well you seem to get along with the kids. I've been thinking about Susan's desire to return to work. I'm trying to understand. But unfortunately I'm from the old school. I still think mommies should stay home with the children and bake cookies and the whole bit. But maybe I need to get liberated. Anyway, what I'm trying to say is, I'm sorry and I hope you'll stay. Now I need to go talk to Susan." But Jessica had already spotted the edge of Susan's blue bathrobe in the hallway.

"You mean it?" asked Susan, running to David. "You'll let me go back to work?" He nodded and they embraced. Jessica sighed in relief.

"Now, Mr. Jerred, you finish your movie and then brush your teeth, because it's after your bedtime," David announced.

"I'm sorry," said Jessica. "I wasn't sure—"

"That's okay. I usually get them to bed. It's my fault," David explained.

"How about Ashley—when does she go to bed?" Jessica asked Susan.

"Oh, about the same time as Jerred, right David?" Susan looked to her husband for confirmation.

"That's right. See Jessica, we have this set up. I put them to bed, since Susan has to get up in the night with Ashley. Besides, it's kind of a special time for me with my kids."

Jessica nodded. She'd never seen a dad like this. Where she'd come from, children were always the mother's responsibility. She wondered what her brother Danny would say if April made him take care of the baby.

"So, is there anything else you'd like me to do?" asked Jessica. Susan had already disappeared down the hallway.

"No thanks, Jessica. I'll hook up the intercom in your room later—that way you can hear Ashley," said David. He was already warming a bottle for the baby.

Jessica closed the door to her tiny windowless room. It really looked more like a storage room, but at least it was her own space. She hung up her few articles of clothing in the tiny closet and sat on the narrow bed. The walls were stark white, and the room was empty except for the bed. She looked at her watch; it was almost ten, but for some reason she wasn't sleepy. Besides, David was going to hook up the intercom.

She went into the pint-sized bathroom next to her room. Jessica had never had her very own bathroom. She stood before the sink and stared at the mirror. Another strange image met her, no longer the bleached-blond sophisticate wanna-be. With her old hair color back, she looked respectable again. But who was *this* Jessica? She ran her fingers through her hair and put her face close to the mirror. Where did she fit?

Back in her room, she dug out a wrinkled postcard to write to Todd. So far she hadn't let on to him about Seattle; she'd only mentioned she might write to her mother. She hadn't written her family for nearly a week. She knew they would wonder why she wasn't in New York anymore, but what would they think if they knew she was here?

Dear Todd, she began. *You'll probably be surprised to learn I'm in Seattle with my mother. She's wonderful and wants me to live with her. I think I will. She's got two darling kids and her husband is a lawyer. They are pretty well off. Seattle is nice. Please give Zephyr a carrot for me and tell the folks "hi." I'll write to everyone later. Sincerely, Jess.* She knew it wasn't exactly the truth, but at least they wouldn't worry about her. A knock interrupted her thoughts.

"Jessica, I want to install that intercom," David called. He came in with a small drill, made a hole, and pulled some wires through. Then he attached a little box with a knob and showed her how to turn it on. "I think Ashley only awakens once, usually around three A.M. The pediatrician says she should be sleeping through the night by now, but I think Ashley has her own ideas about these things." He looked around the sparse room. "Wow, this room is tiny. We have a guest room. But I guess Susan wants you in here. But it is pretty claustrophobic. Do you need anything? You sure didn't bring much stuff. . . . I suppose you'll bring more later—"

"The room's fine," she said, cutting him off. "But a chair might be nice." David nodded and left. She hoped he wouldn't ask too many questions about her, like where she was from or anything. She would collaborate with Susan tomorrow.

Jessica washed some things in the tiny bathroom and hung them to dry across the shower door. Her mattress was stiff and hard, but now she had become so tired she hardly noticed. It seemed she had barely fallen asleep when a strange whining sound awoke her. Ashley! She leaped out of bed and hurried to the baby's room, wondering how long she had been crying. She turned on the nursery lamp and crib. The tape on her disposable diaper had come undone.

"I'm sorry, sweety. Are you hungry?" Ashley clung to Jessica and continued to cry. "Shh, shh," hushed Jessica as she changed her from head to toe, then tiptoed to the kitchen to warm a bottle.

She settled with Ashley in the rocker in the family room. A light glowed softly from above the kitchen stove, giving the room a soft, cozy look. Ashley drank contentedly, and Jessica wiped the baby's wet cheeks with her fingertip. Before the bottle was empty Ashley was asleep again. But Jessica continued to rock her. It was a nice feeling holding a sleeping baby in her arms. Jessica had never thought she liked little kids much, and she always tried to get out of baby-sitting, except for the church nursery. Everyone always assumed a teenaged girl should want to baby-sit. But, she had always preferred to feed stock, clean stalls, or drive a tractor. That was better than taking care of someone else's runny-nosed kids. At least until now. . . . For some reason these two were already becoming important to her. Maybe it was because they were actually her flesh-and-blood relatives.

She tucked the serene baby into the crib and turned off the nursery lamp. The house was silent; everyone was sleeping peacefully. She went back to her room and lay in bed, wide awake now. She wondered if she would really send that card to Todd. It sounded pretty smug and self-satisfied. Would it burn her last bridge?

12

"Jessie," whispered Jerred. "Ya gonna get up now, Jessie?" He stood barefoot by her bed, his little hand resting on her arm. She looked at her watch. Six-thirty. This would've been considered sleeping in back on the farm.

"Sure, I'm getting up," she yawned. "Jerred, you go play quietly in the family room while I take a quick shower, then I'll fix you some breakfast, okay?" He nodded. She listened to the intercom, and the even breathing told her the baby still slept. She jumped in and out of the shower in less than five minutes, pulled on her clothes, and went to see what Jerred was up to. She found him standing on the kitchen counter with a box of sugary cereal in his hands.

"Jerred, what are you doing? I told you I'd be right out."

He looked at her in surprise. "Yeah, that's what Mommy always says. You're fast, Jessie." She laughed and ran her fingers through her damp hair. Jerred still clutched the bright-colored box of cereal with one arm half buried.

"Ugh, are you going to eat that?" she asked.

"Uh-huh. I always eat Sugar Goons." He stirred his hand around in the box and dug deeper. "There's a s'prise in here." Cereal began to overflow from the box and onto the counter.

"Jerred, you want me for a nanny, right?" Jessica tapped her toe on the tile floor with impatience. He nodded and continued to dig, spilling more cereal. "Well, as your nanny, I won't allow you to eat that stuff. You need a good breakfast. Now, you clean up this mess and we'll see what we can find." She confiscated the box, and Jerred picked up the colorful Sugar Goons, one by one, off the blue tile counter and popped them into his mouth. She giggled and opened the refrigerator. It was a big fancy one, with water and ice right in the door, the kind her Kansas Mom had always wished for. But this refrigerator, unlike the one in Kansas, was nearly empty. There were a few eggs and half a carton of milk. She found some stale bread and started fixing French toast. Jerred watched in fascination as she mixed the batter and laid the soggy slices of bread in the sizzling, buttered pan. The baby began to cry.

"Don't touch a thing," she ordered and dashed off to get Ashley. She grabbed a diaper and carried Ashley back to the kitchen, then flipped the toast with her free hand. She quickly changed the baby right in the kitchen. She wasn't sure if that was a good idea, but she was trying not to let the toast burn. She tossed the diaper in the garbage and quickly washed her hands.

"Wow, you are good!" exclaimed David. "And something smells delicious." He picked up Ashley and placed her in the high chair.

"Oh, hi, want some? I wasn't sure if you guys got up this early. But there's plenty." She was beginning to like David a little. His first impression hadn't been so hot, but she realized it was only because he cared about his kids.

"Great, I'll make some coffee. I think there's maple syrup in the pantry." He seemed right at home in the kitchen, and Jessica tried to stay out of his way. She warmed a bottle for Ashley and handed it to her in the high chair. After Ashley finished, she banged it on the metal tray, over and over.

"Enough of that, Ashley," Jessica scolded good-naturedly. "I'll bet you want some real food, don't you?" She found some strained applesauce and spooned it into Ashley's mouth, between flipping the French toast.

"I want some applesauce too," whined Jerred.

"Jerred, you get to have big-boy food," Jessica explained. "Here, bring me your plate and I'll give you some." He complied and watched with big blue eyes as she laid two thick slices on his plate. "Can you eat that much?" she asked.

"Yep, I'm a big boy." He set his plate on the table and climbed up into his chair.

"Should I make some for Susan?" asked Jessica as she finally got to her own plate.

"Nah, Susan usually sleeps in," David said. "Good French toast, Jessie." He flipped the page of his paper and sipped his coffee. Jessica sat down and thought how pleasant it was to eat breakfast family-style. It had been a long time.

Later that morning, David took Jerred to run errands. Jessica dressed Ashley in a pair of overalls and took her out in the backyard. It was a nice backyard, but the flower beds were overgrown with weeds. She dragged a dusty playpen out of the garage, wiped it down, and placed it in the shade for Ashley. In a little shed, she located some rusty garden tools and a pair of old garden gloves. It felt good to get close to the earth. And even though it was the end of July, Seattle's weather was nothing like Kansas. It was warm and humid, but quite bearable.

After a while, Susan stepped out on the deck and stretched luxuriantly, still in her bathrobe. She sipped her coffee and smiled. "What a beautiful day! I feel so good. I haven't had a solid night's sleep for just . . . forever." Jessica smiled and tugged hard on a particularly stubborn weed.

"You know, Jessica, I still can't quite believe it. I mean that you're actually my daughter." She sat down on a smooth wooden deck chair. "I guess after I gave you up, I just sort of washed you from my memory. Now here you are, a grown woman—well, almost. It makes me feel rather old."

Jessica laid down the spade. "Well, you don't look old, Susan. I'm sure no one would believe you're actually my mother." Jessica brushed the dirt off her jeans and joined Susan on the deck. "But, I'm worried, Susan. David might be curious about my past, and I don't know what to say. I don't really want to lie. . . ."

"Hmm . . ." Susan sipped her coffee and looked across the yard. "Well, tell him you're from Kansas—that's not a lie. Say you just graduated from high school and came out to Washington to stay with relatives. See, that's not completely a lie either. And then you needed work, so you applied to be a nanny. There—it's simple."

Ashley started to fuss. "I think she's hungry," said Jessica. "It's been a couple hours since she ate."

After Jessica fed and changed the baby, she returned to the backyard, but Susan was nowhere in sight. Jessica picked up the hoe and started to weed around the rhododendrons.

"My goodness," David exclaimed as he came through the gate. "What are you? Nanny, cook, house-cleaner, and gardener, too? We better not let this get around, Jessie. Someone will offer you better wages and steal you away."

Jessica smiled. "Oh, it's kind of relaxing to be outside, and you have such a pretty yard. It's funny, though, I never enjoyed yard work that much at home." Jerred came tearing around the corner of the house.

"Jessie, come see! Come see!" he squealed, grabbing her hand and hauling her to the driveway. In the back of the shiny Jeep Cherokee sat a cardboard box. Inside was a small brown puppy.

"I can't believe I did it," whispered David. "Susan's going to kill me. But Jerred met a kid in front of the hardware store. Smart kid too—he handed the puppy right over to

Jerred before I could say anything. I noticed a sign that said 'Puppies for sale,' only the for sale part was crossed out and it said 'free.' I guess the rest is obvious. Actually, we paid the boy, and it seems like a nice little mutt. The kid said he's a cross between a cocker and a terrier."

"He's darling." Jessica scooped up the chocolate-colored pup from the box and looked into his big, lucid eyes. "Does he need shots or anything?"

"Yes, I'm sure he needs everything. In fact, I told Jerred he can't play with him until we take him to a vet. We'll have to keep him in the garage over the weekend."

"Well, I've always heard mutts make the best pets," Jessica commented as she placed him gently back in the box.

———

Susan threw a small fit about the puppy. Jessica was in Ashley's room and tried not to listen, but the room was right next to the master bedroom. Ashley, oblivious to her parents' dispute, sat up in her crib with an endearing smile and extended her chubby little arms. Jessica grabbed a dry diaper and quickly moved the baby to the family room, where Jerred was busily building a long road with wooden blocks.

"Jessie, when do I get to play with my puppy?" he asked.

"Jerred, your dad already told you. He has to go to the vet first, to make sure everything's okay. He'll be fine in the garage for now. Have you thought of a name for him yet?"

"No, let's think of a name, Jessie." He held up a block. "How 'bout Block?"

Jessica frowned. "I bet you can think of another name." She racked her brain. "Let's see, there must be lots of good dog names. He's brown, so you could call him Brownie, or Cocoa, or Chestnut, or Mahogany—" She was really on a roll.

"Brownie! Brownie! Yep, I like it, Jessica. I'm gonna call

him Brownie!" He said the name again and again in a sing-song voice.

"Jessica," called Susan. "I'm going out to get groceries and do some shopping. I know there's not much to work with, but see if you can find something for lunch, okay? See you."

"I'm hungry, Jessica," Jerred whined.

Jessica looked around the room where the blocks had been strewn by Jerred's Brownie dance. "Well, you pick these up and I'll see what I can find." She knew there wasn't much in the fridge but found some hot dogs.

"You're in luck, partner." Jessica held up the package.

"I don't wanna hot dog," he complained.

Jessica shook her head. "What do you mean? Last night it was the only thing you'd eat."

"It made my tummy hurt." He looked up with innocent eyes, and Jessica wasn't sure if he was pulling one over on her or not.

"I have an idea," announced David, plucking up Ashley and setting her high on his shoulders. She giggled and cooed and drooled right down the side of his face. Jessica handed him a paper towel. "Thanks. Now for my idea. Since Jessie made such a nice breakfast and even weeded the yard, I think we should take her out to Hamburger Chuck's for lunch."

"Yippee!" yelled Jerred. He zipped out of the kitchen and returned shortly with a big cowboy hat. "I'm rip ready to go!"

They piled into the Cherokee, and David turned on the radio. It was tuned to a country station, which made Jessica almost feel at home. The restaurant was western-style, with cowboy memorabilia and giant buckeroo burgers.

"This place is great!" exclaimed Jessica between bites.

"Yep, we cowboys like to come here every once in a while," said David, winking at Jerred. Ashley sat in a high chair and sucked on a French fry.

"You know, Jerred," Jessica said in a serious tone. "One of my brothers is a real-live cowboy."

"Really?" Jerred's eyes grew wide.

"Yeah, and he has two cutting horses and rides in real rodeos. But his best event is bronc-riding."

Jerred's eyes grew wider. "Wow! Does his horse cut with real scissors?" They laughed, and David explained to Jerred about cutting horses. Jessica was impressed with David's knowledge about rodeos. She knew he was an important attorney, but for the moment he seemed like an ordinary guy, like one of her own brothers.

"I've even been in a couple of local rodeos," said Jessica. "They're pretty small, but still lots of fun."

"So, what rodeo event do you do?" David asked with genuine interest.

"Oh, just barrel racing, and I'm not that good. My horse is a little on the big side and not as fast as some, but it was always fun."

"You have a horse, too?" asked Jerred in amazement. "Can I ride your horse, Jessie?"

She laughed, but her laugh sounded hollow. "No, sorry little buckeroo. My horse, Zephyr's his name, lives back in Kansas."

"I didn't know you were from Kansas," said David. "Of course, now that you mention it, you do have a little bit of a midwestern drawl or something."

The restaurant was next to a shopping mall and they strolled around a bit after lunch. Jessica and Jerred went into a small card shop, where Jessica purchased some stationery and stamps. She wanted to write to Joanna and Celeste and maybe Todd again.

When they got home, Susan was already unloading the groceries. Jessica helped put things away and listened to Susan complain about how crowded the store was and how it all took so long.

"I've got an idea, Susan," began David. "Remember that old bed and breakfast up on Fox Island?"

"Uh-huh. What about it?"

"Why don't I call and see if they have a room? With Jessie here, you and I could take the ferry over and spend the night. What do you say?"

"Oh, I don't know. I wanted to have tomorrow free to get ready for work."

He groaned. "Oh, come on, it doesn't take a whole day to get ready for work. We haven't gone off just the two of us since Ashley was born. What do you think, Jessie? Is it okay with you?"

"Fine," said Jessica. She was feeling pretty confident now but wondered if it was really such a good idea. Of course, Susan knew that she wasn't a real nanny.

"Come on, Susan, we'll have a terrific time!" urged David.

"Oh, okay," Susan agreed reluctantly. "I'll go pack, but you better check the ferry schedules."

Within the hour, they were gone. The house was strangely quiet and calm, both children napping. Jessica continued to put the abandoned groceries away and straighten up the kitchen. Soon everything was spick-and-span. She wandered down the hall to the master bedroom and wondered if they would appreciate a quick pick-up in there too. Or would that be invading their privacy? She pushed open the door and peeked in to discover a spacious room in complete disarray. At first she supposed it was due to their quick departure, but as she straightened she realized it was at least a week's worth of neglected accumulation. She sorted and straightened and the laundry pile grew. The luxurious master bath was sadly neglected. She scoured the stained grout between the tiles with a discarded toothbrush.

She wanted to make it shine. She wanted to please Susan, and perhaps win her approval. She changed the sheets on the king-sized bed, then noticed more blankets and pillows arranged on the chaise lounge as if someone had recently slept there. But by the time she had finished, the room could have been photographed for *Better Homes and Gardens*. She even picked some flowers and placed them in a crystal vase on Susan's dresser. Finally, she gathered up the laundry and loaded the washer just as a familiar cry sounded.

As she hurried toward the baby's room, an uncomfortable thought struck her. What was she doing? Why was she working her tail off while other kids her age were out having a good time? Was it really worth it? It would be if Susan would accept her. Besides, she was used to hard work. Of course, she could usually look forward to a good time at the end of the day—a movie, a pizza with friends, or even a ride on Zephyr.

Ashley stood in her crib, arms outstretched, eagerly awaiting an escape, and Jessica temporarily forgot her concern. They played and ate dinner, and bedtime went fairly smooth. Brownie whined once in a while out in the garage, and Jessica went out and held him, promising him he would soon get to come inside.

Finally, Jessica finished the last load of clothes and fell into bed exhausted. But three A.M. came fast, and she barely managed to drag herself out of bed to attend to Ashley.

Once again, Jerred woke her up at six-thirty. He seemed to have an inborn alarm clock. She and Jerred had just sat down to eggs and toast when Ashley's cries floated down the hallway. Jessica slowly got up, her tiredness and exasperation starting to show as she threw down her napkin.

"Why don't you just let her cry?" said Jerred with a full mouth.

"That would be mean," replied Jessica, but thinking it sounded like a good idea.

"Mommy just lets her cry lots of times. You don't have to get her, Jessie." She headed for Ashley's room anyway, but Jerred ran ahead and blocked the doorway with his arms spread wide and his feet straddled.

"Jerred, you need to move so I can get your sister."

"No, just let her cry and cry and cry! We don't need her, anyway. She's just a crybaby, and I hate her!" Jessica removed him from the door and lifted Ashley from her crib.

"I hate you, Jessie!" he screamed. "I wish you'd just go away." Jerred ran to his room and slammed the door, and Jessica wondered what to do. She tended to the baby and then gently knocked on Jerred's door.

"I'm not home!" he yelled.

"I think you are, Jerred." She opened the door. "Can I come in?" He said nothing, but she could see his toes sticking out from under the bed. She crawled under to join him. "Hey, this is pretty cool down here, Jerred. But that sandwich looks kind of old and yucky. I hope you weren't thinking of eating it for breakfast." Jerred giggled. "In fact, I bet our breakfast is getting cold—don't you want to come eat with me? Ashley's all happy now, but she can't sit at the table and talk to me like you can. Oh well, I guess I'll just have to eat alone." She scooted out from under the bed.

"Do you still like me, Jessie?"

"Of course, you silly. I need you to be a big boy and help me with Ashley. It's not easy taking care of a baby. If you could just help me a little, we could have lots more fun."

"Really?" He slipped his hand in hers.

"Really. There're lots of things you could help with, Jerred. Today, we'll have to work them out, okay?"

Jerred helped straighten Ashley's room, and Jessica showed him how to fold washcloths and match socks. He got pretty good at it and even had fun. Later they took a walk around the neighborhood, and Jerred pushed Ashley's stroller.

While the kids napped, Jessica straightened the house again and cut some pretty flowers for a bouquet on the dining room table. She decided to fix a nice dinner for when Susan and David got home. She started by making a fruit salad and setting the table, but then Jerred and the baby awoke and needed attention. She put rice on to cook and then played a game with Jerred. The timer went off, and Jessica promised to read him a story if he would watch Ashley while she put the chicken on to broil. They had just opened the book when Susan and David walked in.

"Something smells good in here," said David. He swooped up Jerred and stroked Ashley's smooth round head.

"It's after seven, David!" Susan snapped without even greeting Jessica or her kids. "I told you we should've caught the noon ferry. Now I've got so much to do. I don't want any dinner." She stormed off to her room.

"Well, I'm sure hungry," said David. "How about you, little man? Have you worked up a big appetite?"

"Yep, and I'm helping Jessie. She's fixing dinner, and I'm watching baby Ashley."

They sat down to eat, but Susan's chair was once again empty. Jessica studied David's face; he looked sad. She had hoped their getaway would return them happy and refreshed. She hadn't noticed before, but David was pretty good-looking for an older guy. She wondered how old he was—probably late-thirties—but he still had a sweet boyish look about him, with his bright blue eyes and sandy hair. She couldn't help but wonder why Susan was so mean to him.

13

"Good morning, everyone," announced Susan with a cheerful smile. "Isn't it a fantastic day?" Jessica and Jerred looked up from their oatmeal in surprise. Susan poured coffee, glanced distastefully at the leftover oatmeal still in the pan, then headed out the door. So far Jessica hadn't seen Susan eat much of anything besides diet soda and coffee. But Susan, petite and slender, did look nice in her new linen suit.

David emerged with Ashley draped over an arm and a briefcase under the other. "She still needs changing, but I rescued her for you." He handed her over to Jessica. "I'm already late for an early appointment, and I still need to drop the pup at the vet's. See you, Jessie." He kissed Jerred on the top of the head and went out the door.

"Will my mommy ride to work with Daddy today?" asked Jerred with his mouth full of oatmeal.

"I guess so." Jessica peeked out. Sure enough, Susan was sitting behind the wheel of the BMW with David beside her. "Yep, there they go." Jessica wondered why Susan didn't even tell Jerred goodbye. Did she think it would be too traumatic for him?

"Mommy used to go to work with Daddy all the time," said Jerred as he scraped the bowl with his spoon and licked it clean.

"Where did you stay when your mommy went to work, Jerred?"

"At Peggy's. Before that I went to Kiddy-Care—it was

147

yucky there. But Peggy was nice, except for Johnny."

"Johnny?"

"The mean boy," he answered, as if that explained everything. Jessica nodded in understanding.

The day progressed smoothly. Jessica was getting the kids into something of a routine, and most of the time it actually worked. Kids, she decided, weren't a whole lot different than livestock. Both her chores on the farm and in the house had proved good training ground for being a nanny.

Later that afternoon, she started dinner. She hoped Susan might join them for a change. She wanted so badly to impress Susan, to make her want to get to know Jessica and appreciate her.

"Is Daddy bringing Brownie back today?" asked Jerred.

"Uh-huh," Jessica answered as she drained the hot pasta over the sink. She heard a car and looked out the steamy window to see the BMW in the drive. David got out with the puppy, and Susan slammed her door and stomped into the house.

"I won't have that dog in my house!" she yelled. "Do you hear? He has to stay in the garage!"

"Brownie! Brownie!" cried Jerred, jumping to pet his puppy.

"Hold on there, little man," said David, laying down his briefcase. "The vet says Brownie needs to be kept quiet and checked regularly. He's having a reaction to one of the shots."

"He could stay in my room," offered Jessica. "I could take care of him." Susan scowled and Jessica cringed. Lately, every time she tried to be helpful it seemed to backfire.

"Would you mind, Jessie? Of course, we could just put him back in the garage. . . ."

"No, it's fine with me. That is if Susan doesn't care." Jessica looked hopefully into Susan's gray eyes. They looked like a storm brewing.

"No, go right ahead!" said Susan sharply, turning on her

heel. "That room's practically not part of this house anyway. It's a good place for a dog!"

Jessica carefully removed the pup from David's arms and carried him back to her room. Susan's words stung. Jessica clenched her teeth to avoid tears of anger. Jerred followed at her heels, and soon David returned with a new wicker dog bed and shiny new dishes.

"I picked these up during lunch," said David.

"How about the corner by the closet?" Jessica suggested. She gently laid Brownie on the red plaid cushion.

David glanced around the tiny cubicle. "Sorry about Susan. I think she was just tired. I also think this room is over its capacity limit. Maybe we should see about the guest room."

Jessica put the finishing touches on dinner, and Susan actually sat down with them. Still she only picked at her food. Jessica wondered if it was her cooking. She had learned from her mom on the farm. Maybe Susan was just finicky. Ashley fussed and cried, and soon Jessica removed her from the table.

Rocking the baby in the nursery, Jessica wondered when she would get some time off. So far it seemed she'd worked nonstop around the clock. But what bothered her even more was Susan's complete lack of appreciation.

When Jessica returned to the dining room, she found a deserted table full of dirty dishes. The cold spaghetti was stuck to her plate. She ate it anyway, then cleared the table. David and Jerred wrestled in the family room. But their laughter was a good sound.

In Susan's well-lit kitchen, Jessica mechanically scraped and rinsed the dinner plates. At least there weren't many. Nothing compared to the farm. Not only that, Susan had a dishwasher. Jessica wondered what Susan could be doing now. She wished they could talk.

"Need some help?" David offered. "That was a great dinner, Jessie. I'm starting to think Susan is right about returning to work." He vigorously scrubbed a pot. "You see,

Susan has always worked—in fact, that's how we met. She only took six weeks maternity leave when Jerred was born. But I figured when Ashley came along, Susan might as well stay home with the kids for a while. The way I see it, to pay child care for two kids and keep a maid is not very sensible, not to mention Susan always needs a new wardrobe when she works. Anyway, maybe I was wrong."

Jessica wondered. She dried the last pot and hung the dish towel. She was ready for a break. Just then the baby cried, and Jessica wanted to cry too.

"Never mind about Ashley, Jessie. Why don't you call it a day—you look beat. Hey, by the way, thanks for the cleanup in our bedroom. It sure needed it."

She blushed. "Oh, I hope you don't mind. I was just trying to help out. David, I noticed your bookshelf in the den. Do you mind if I borrow a book?"

"No, just make yourself completely at home." He smiled, and the corners of his eyes crinkled boyishly.

Jessica found an Agatha Christie paperback and went to check on Brownie. He slept peacefully in his snug little bed as she put away her clean laundry. She tried to enjoy a long, relaxing shower. She didn't even listen for Jerred's little taps on the door.

After her shower, she returned to her room to discover a dark blue easy chair wedged into a corner. She recognized it from David's den. Behind the chair stood a floor lamp at a perfect height for reading. A little oak table was next to her bed with a clock radio on it. Folded neatly across the foot of her bed was a pretty wool blanket in shades of blue and mauve. Now her tiny windowless room almost looked homey. She wished it had been the effort of her mother, but she knew it must have been David. Susan had probably put her foot down about the guest room idea, and David was trying to make up for it. She sank into the comfy chair and picked up the book, but she could no longer focus her eyes.

The week progressed, each day much like the previous ones. Except for the time Jerred cut his head when he fell off the backyard swing. Jessica had held a cold washcloth on it until David rushed home and whisked him off to the doctor. Jerred proudly returned with four stitches and a sucker. That was when Jessica mentioned she was a pretty good driver, if they trusted her enough to leave the keys.

"Oh sure, Jessie," agreed David. "You know, I never even thought about it. But you could take the Cherokee out if you need to."

During the weekend, Susan was as evasive as ever. At this rate, Jessica would never get to know her. She was starting to feel trapped by this deal. It appeared Susan really had no interest in getting acquainted. Still, Jessica had come to love the children, and David was wonderful. But what was she really doing here?

On Sunday, David wanted to take his family down to the waterfront to see a restored clipper ship that was docked for the day. Jerred leaped around pretending to be a pirate, with Brownie nipping at his heels like a bouncy little shadow.

"Sorry, I've got a million things to do this afternoon," Susan declined. "Why don't you take Jessica and the kids?" David looked at Jessica. It was the same expression Jerred used when he wanted her to read a story.

"Sure, I'd love to come!" she exclaimed. Any reason to get out of the house was welcome to her. "Let me get Ashley ready."

"Great, I'll pack the stroller. Come on, Jerred, you can help me."

Down on the waterfront, Jessica stared at the Sound in amazement; it was the first time she'd seen it up close. They investigated the ship from stem to stern for over an hour and finally had to pry Jerred off. Then they strolled through the waterfront shops, admiring the various handicrafts. David

bought Jerred a wooden paddle wheel boat that was pro-
pelled by a large rubberband.

Jessica admired a pair of shell earrings set in sterling at a
jewelry kiosk. They got some smoked salmon and ate shrimp
cocktails from small paper cups while they walked. People
smiled and admired the children, and Jessica wondered if they
looked like a family. She enjoyed that grown-up feeling. She
imagined she was really David's wife and the mother of these
two. But her charade was spoiled by twinges of guilt. What
would David think if he could read her mind? Of course she
wouldn't really want to replace Susan. Not really.

They sat down to fish and chips at a grubby picnic table
garnished with big white sea gull splats. Jessica gave Ashley
a bottle and held the blanket to shield the baby from a cool
sea breeze just starting to blow. She sipped her lemonade
from the waxy cup and noticed Jerred and David whispering about something. Then Jerred shyly approached her,
not like his usual boisterous self. He handed her a little white
box with a blue sea gull embossed on the lid. Inside,
wrapped in tissue, were the pretty shell earrings. She looked
up to David in surprise, and both he and Jerred grinned like
naughty school boys.

"Put 'em on, Jessie!" urged Jerred. She thanked them,
then awkwardly held the baby and slipped them on. She felt
David's eyes upon her, and suddenly she wondered if he
had guessed her earlier thoughts. Her cheeks burned and
she couldn't look up. She couldn't bear to look into his clear
blue gaze. What if he knew? What if he thought she was
making some sort of a move on him?

———

The next few days Jessica avoided David. At the same
time, she found herself thinking about him a lot and felt
ashamed for it. When he looked at her, she felt even more
uncomfortable. She wondered if he might have had similar

thoughts. The guilt and the turmoil were eating her up inside. She knew she couldn't go on like this. She was making herself crazy. It was useless to try talking to Susan about anything; how could she bring herself to tell her mother she might have a crush on her husband? To make matters worse, she'd started watching those silly daytime talk shows. They made things like this seem real—it was always some guy's dad had stolen his girlfriend, or someone's sister-in-law was dating their son. It was so demented. She could just imagine herself with Susan on Jenny Jones. Susan would be saying, *"My daughter put the move on my husband when I invited her into my home."*

Finally one evening, after a particularly trying day of fighting with her emotions and trying to keep up with the kids, she watched as the BMW pulled into the driveway. David hopped out and opened the door for Susan. She stepped out with a big smile, and he pulled her towards him and hugged her. It was a long embrace, finished with a kiss. Suddenly Jessica realized with relief, as well as a teeny stab of jealousy, it had only been her imagination, at least as far as David was concerned. She sighed and felt as if a heavy weight had been lifted.

Things fell into a normal pattern again. Try as she would, Jessica could not seem to get Susan to talk to her. It was as if Susan was avoiding her.

Brownie managed to get into everything, but in the evenings Jessica tried to keep him out of trouble and out of Susan's sight. It was hard not to spoil the sweet little pup, especially when he looked up with those liquid brown eyes. Jerred and Brownie had become inseparable friends. Jerred even sneaked him into bed at night.

On Thursday morning, a letter arrived from Todd. Of course, he had figured it out. He was the one who had given her Susan's address. She quickly scanned for the latest farm news: how busy they were, how much he missed her, and how he wished she'd come home. She clenched her teeth and tucked the letter into her jeans pocket. Later at the park, as Jerred played in the sandbox and Ashley slept in her stroller, she took time to read it more carefully. This time Jessica laughed when she read the part about Todd going to the coffeehouse and how the crowd really got into C.S. Lewis. Leave it to Todd. Suddenly she missed him, missed Kansas, missed Zephyr and everyone like she had never missed them before. She knew it was harvest time now; everyone would be busier than ever. They'd probably miss her, too, out there driving the combine. She'd always been a good combine driver, careful and patient, cutting the corners just the way Dad liked.

"Jessie, I'm thirsty," whined Jerred, wiping his sandy little hands on her white jeans.

"Yeah, me too." She looked in her purse. All she had was a dollar and some change. Susan still hadn't paid her, and Jessica wasn't sure if she ever meant to. They had never talked about wages. At first, Jessica figured she would just be helping out, like a member of the family. But in reality, Susan treated her more like a slave than a relative, let alone a daughter.

"C'mon, Jessie. Let's get somethin' to drink." They walked over to the vendor and Jessica had just enough for two sodas.

Somehow, David had enticed Susan to drive up to British Colombia with him for the weekend. They would attend a wedding and visit his folks. Ashley had a cold, so Jessica offered to stay home with the kids.

By Sunday afternoon, the house was a disaster. Jessica let kids and pup run wild. She had hardly picked up a single thing all weekend. She sat beside Jerred on the couch and surveyed the damage.

"Well, Jerred, looks like we better get busy if we're going to get this cleaned up before your parents get home."

"Are you my mommy, Jessie?" asked Jerred unexpectedly.

"No, of course not. You know that, silly." She poked him playfully in the tummy.

"You feel like my mommy, Jessie. Like that book we read today. You love me and take care of me. That's what a mommy does. Right?"

Jessica thought about it. *Mommy*. What did it mean? Who was her mother? Maybe Jerred was right. Maybe it was the one who cared for you, the one who loved you. She pictured her mom—the one in Kansas—sweltering in front of a hot kitchen stove in August, cooking for the harvest crew. She would be frumpy and tired, but still willing to listen if Jessica needed an ear. She was a strong woman in her own way. She was devoted to her family, always ready to work hard and make home a better place. Then it became clear. She knew in her heart who her mother was.

But what about poor Jerred and Ashley? They were so hungry for nurturing and mothering. Susan didn't seem to understand. Did Jessica, as their half sister, owe them something?

"We better get busy, Jerred." She left his question dangling in the air. She knew no answer that could satisfy them both.

That night she wrote a letter to her family. For the first time, she told them all that she was sorry. She told them how much they meant to her. That was all she said. No promises. No lies.

The next week plodded along. Jessica decided to bring up the subject of money but didn't quite know how. Susan rarely joined them for dinner, and Jessica seldom saw her alone, and then only briefly for exchanges of information, directions, and what not. But never a word of encouragement, a mention of gratitude. Jessica knew she was being taken for granted by Susan. But even worse, it seemed like Susan resented her too.

David, as usual, tried to be sweet and helpful. He tried to make up for Susan by being a perfect daddy. Sometimes Jessica felt as if she were sitting on an active volcano, ready to blow at any moment. She wasn't sure which one of them would go off first. She was afraid it might be her.

———

"You'll have to take the Cherokee today, David," Susan announced Friday morning as she grabbed a diet soda from the fridge. "Rhonda got tickets for the theater and I'm going with her tonight."

"When will you be home?" David stooped over and peeled Jerred from his back.

"I don't know—depends on how late the show is. I might spend the night with Rhonda." Susan brushed a piece of imaginary lint off her skirt and exited.

"We can talk about it at work. All right tiger, you've had it!" exclaimed David, and he galloped across the room, dumped Jerred on the couch, and tickled him into fits.

Jessica watched them leave in their separate cars. She wondered how they had gotten together in the first place. They seemed like such totally different people. She shook her head and began to sweep the white-tiled floor. Jerred raced through with Brownie at his heels, scattering her dust pile across the kitchen.

"Look, mister!" she said in her tough voice. "If you'd help out a little, maybe we could take a picnic to the park today."

"Yippee! Can we take Brownie too?"

"Oh, I don't know. Maybe he should stay home. Your dad took the Cherokee, and we'll have to walk. That's a long way for his little legs."

"Please, Jessie. He wants to come too. Pleeease?"

"Well, okay. But we'll have to keep him on a leash."

"Yippee!"

Brownie tugged and jerked on his bright red leash. Finally, he tangled it around the wheels of the stroller and nearly dumped Ashley.

"Hey, Jerred, give me a hand," said Jessica as she unwound the leash. "You push Ashley, okay?"

"No, I wanna hold the leash," he whined.

"I better hold it, Jerred. Brownie's still not used to this. You push the baby; you're so good at that."

When they reached the park, Jessica noticed Ashley's seat belt had come undone from her stroller.

"Here, Jerred. Hold the leash, okay?" She squatted down to fix the strap. Just then, Jerred shrieked and darted for the street. Jessica leaped out and grabbed him by an overall suspender. The brakes on a white car screeched, and they looked over to see the little brown pup lying lifeless on the pavement.

"BROWNIE!" screamed Jerred. "My doggy! Is he okay, Jessie? Is Brownie okay?" Jessica's legs went wobbly and her stomach churned at the sight of the obviously dead animal. She sat down on the curb next to Ashley's stroller and pulled Jerred to her. He tried to get away to see his puppy.

"I'm so sorry, dear," said a shaking middle-aged lady, emerging from the car. "I couldn't stop. Thank God you grabbed your little boy. But I didn't even see the doggy until it was too late. I'm so sorry. Whatever can I do?" Jessica just shook her head and a tear trickled down her cheek.

"I want my dog!" screamed Jerred. "I want Brownie!" A small crowd gathered to witness the scene. Jessica wished they would all leave.

"Jerred," she said softly, then more firmly, "Jerred, Brownie is dead. He ran into the street. The street's not a place to play, you know that, Jerred."

"I wanna see him!" demanded Jerred. Jessica looked up at the lady for advice.

"Why not let him see his dog?" she offered. Her face was wet with tears. "It might help him to understand better." Traffic had stopped now, and Jessica walked over with Jerred. He knelt down in the street and stroked Brownie's soft brown coat now misshapen and streaked with blood. He burst into sobs.

A man in a delivery suit brought over a cardboard box. "Here, you can put him in this." Jessica looked at the man.

Did he mean for *her* to pick up Brownie's body? Of course, she knew all about death. . . . It happened on the farm. But it was never easy for her. Not like it seemed to be for Dad; he always dealt with these things. Suddenly she longed for Dad's strong hands to pick up the broken dog, but it was up to her now. She bent over and scooped up the limp puppy, still warm, and laid him in the box. She wondered if it had really been easy for Dad. Or had he been, like she was now, only putting up a strong front? Jerred silently watched her with tears streaming down, and Ashley fussed in her stroller on the sidewalk. Jessica wiped the sticky blood from her hands onto her blue jeans and checked on Ashley.

"Can I give you a ride?" offered the lady. "I think I'm able. . . ."

Jessica looked at the woman's trembling hands and wondered. "Maybe I should drive," Jessica suggested. The woman nodded, and Jessica got everyone in, including the box. They drove home in silence.

"Will you be okay now?" Jessica asked the lady after she pulled into the driveway.

"Yes, but can I reimburse you for the puppy?"

"No, I don't think so. It wasn't really your fault."

Jessica set the box in the garage and washed her hands. She gave Ashley a bottle and laid her in her crib. She felt like a sleepwalker, going through the motions without consciousness. She felt void of any more feelings. Jerred was still sitting in the garage, elbows on knees, staring into the open box. She sat down on the cement step beside him but could think of nothing to say. She was tired to the bone. Tired, hopeless, and beaten.

"My grandma in Canada says God takes you when you die," whispered Jerred. "She says if you believe in Jesus, you go to this really nice place—called heaven."

Jessica nodded. "Your grandma sounds like a wise woman."

Jerred shook his head and choked out, "Then how come Brownie's still here? How come he don't go to heaven?"

Jessica swallowed the lump in her throat and put her arm around Jerred's shoulders. "Maybe it's because we need to bury him and have a funeral."

"What's a fun'ral?"

"Well, it's when you remember how special someone was and how much they meant to you. You talk about it and stuff."

"Can we do it, Jessie?" He looked up with sad blue eyes and wrapped his arms around her neck. She held him close and felt as if her insides were being shredded. For the first time since she had run away with Barry, she felt a tiny trickle of thankfulness for her mistake. In an absurd way Barry had brought her to Jerred, her own little brother.

They walked all around the yard, and Jerred finally selected a spot under the apple tree. They took turns digging. Jessica scrounged through the house until she found a better box with a nice solid lid. They wrapped Brownie in a white dishtowel and laid him gently inside. The dirt made sad, hollow thuds as it fell on the box. They got some wooden stakes in the garage and pounded them together to form a lopsided cross, then Jerred stuck it in the ground. Then they gathered flowers from the yard to decorate the tiny grave.

"Should we have a fun'ral now?" asked Jerred. He wiped a dirty hand across his cheek, leaving a dark brown smear.

"Do you want to wait for your parents?"

"Yeah, Daddy liked Brownie. He'd wanna come too."

14

*J*essica pulled out the uneaten sandwiches from their ruined picnic. After a few bites she found neither of them were hungry. Instead she put Jerred down for a nap.

"Jessie," asked Jerred in a small voice. "Will you stay here while I take my nap?"

"Okay, for a while." She sat down on the floor.

"Jessie, what's heaven like?"

She sighed and stretched out across his sky blue rug. *What is heaven like?* She stared blankly at the ceiling, trying to recall the things she'd learned as a child in Sunday school, but she couldn't remember anything very specific about heaven.

"Is it just clouds and stuff?" asked Jerred, not willing to abandon the subject.

"No, I think it's more than that. . . . I think it's a sunny, happy place where you can ride horses and swim all day without getting tired. With beautiful plants and all kinds of interesting animals and everything."

"That sounds good."

"Yeah, but I think it's even more than that," she continued with growing conviction. "I think it's a place where you know that God loves you and forgives you, and you are so happy just to be with Him. . . ." Jessica remembered feeling like that. There were times back on the farm when it was so good to be alive, and God had seemed very real. Would she ever feel like that again?

She glanced over at Jerred and heard the even breathing

of sleep, then she slipped out of his room.

She straightened the house a little, going through the motions without thinking or feeling. She stacked Brownie's bed and food dishes in a corner of the garage, and outside the sky grew dark and gray. In Kansas, this would spell trouble because they would be getting in the grain now. But here in Seattle it was of little consequence. Soon, giant drops splattered loudly on the skylight above the kitchen, and Jessica flipped on a light.

Ashley awoke, and Jessica sat cross-legged on the family room rug, feeding her a bottle. Soon Jerred, still groggy from sleep, wandered in with red-rimmed eyes.

"Jessie," he said hoarsely, watching the rain pelting the big window behind the couch. "Do you think God is crying 'cause Brownie got runned over?"

Jessica thought for a minute. "No, I think God's crying because He knows how sad we are. Brownie's okay now, Jerred."

"Can we still have a fun'ral—even in the rain?" he asked, curling up beside her and laying his head on her knee.

She stroked his wavy hair, and fresh tears filled her eyes. "Sure, Jerred. I think a funeral in the rain is just fine."

"Hello?" called David down the hall. "What have we here?" He shook out his jacket, hung it over a barstool, and approached the threesome. "What's wrong? Why the gloomy faces?"

Jerred ran and leaped into his daddy's arms. "Brownie's dead!" he sobbed. "He got runned over by a car!"

David searched Jessica's face and she nodded, wiping her tears on the back of her hand. It was so silly to cry over a dog. But David's eyes grew misty too, and he turned away with Jerred still in his arms.

"I'm so sorry, little man. You should've called me."

"It's gonna be okay, Daddy," reassured Jerred, sounding like the grown-up now. "Me and Jessie buried him and everything. We're gonna have a fun'ral, but I wanted you to come too."

They stood out in the rain before the muddy little mound and soggy flowers. David and Jessica each said a few words about Brownie, then Jerred finished.

"Dear God, I hope you like Brownie. I'm glad he was my dog. But I sure wish I could have him back. . . . Take care of him. He really likes to play chase."

They left their mucky shoes in a wet pile by the back door, and David dried Jerred's hair with a kitchen towel.

"I think you've had quite a day," said David. "How 'bout I go get us some pizza and a movie?" Jerred smiled a pathetic little smile and David swooped him up. "Want to come with me, little man?" But Jerred glanced at Jessica and shook his head. David looked at her with puzzled eyes. "Okay, Jerred, you stay here and take care of Jessie and Baby Ashley."

"Jessie?" asked Jerred as soon as his dad was gone. "Was it my fault Brownie got runned over?" He looked stricken, as if this horrible thought had just occurred to him.

She wondered how to answer. In a way, she was to blame. She never should have given Jerred the leash in the first place. But maybe it didn't matter. "No, it wasn't really anyone's fault, Jerred. Sometimes things just happen and no one knows why." Ashley's cries interrupted their conversation. "Why don't you come help me with the baby?" He followed her, and she gave him little insignificant things to do, but he did them with an air of importance.

Jessica sat with Ashley in front of the empty fireplace, staring into the cold, black grate. She shivered.

"Will you read me a story?" asked Jerred, holding a book in his hand. Ashley gurgled happily, making loud sucking noises on her bottle.

"Sure, come on over," Jessica invited. She made room on her knee for the book. She looked at the cover and sighed. It would have to be about a dog.

"I'll turn the pages," offered Jerred.

"The Poky Little Puppy," she began, trying to inject enthusiasm into her voice. But inside she felt dead and empty, and as black as the empty fireplace. Finally, she flipped the last page. She felt someone watching and looked up to see David in the hallway, gazing as if mesmerized. He turned away and put the pizza box on the counter along with a bag.

"I didn't know which kind you like, Jessie. So I got the combination."

"Oh, I like almost any kind of pizza. Back home we didn't get it much, and then I had to fight off my brothers."

David grinned and opened the box. Jessica found paper plates and poured some juice. They ate in the family room and David built a big, crackling fire. It seemed odd having a fire in August, but Seattle was like that—some days were hot, others mild, and today was downright chilly.

"What movie did you get, Daddy?" asked Jerred as he stretched a stringy piece of cheese out and sucked it in like spaghetti.

"*The Wizard of Oz.* I haven't seen it since I was a kid, and it just appealed to me tonight."

"Oh, I love that movie!" exclaimed Jessica. "It's been years since I've seen it."

Jessica cleaned up the pizza paraphernalia, David gave Jerred his bath, then they all met back for the movie. For some reason the old movie made her cry. Maybe it was Kansas, or maybe it was Dorothy's plight, painfully similar to her own. Or maybe it was just the little dog, Toto. Today had brought more than a fair share of tears. She sat and cried in front of the fire with her back to David and Jerred. She didn't want to be observed. Jerred fell asleep on the couch during the poppy field scene, and David put Ashley to bed.

At last Dorothy got safely back to Kansas and David turned off the VCR. "Well, did that make you homesick for Kansas, Jessie?" he asked lightly.

"As a matter of fact, it did." Her answer seemed to catch him off guard, and he scratched his head and frowned.

"Just what are your plans for the future, Jessie? I'm not trying to be intrusive—and of course you're a fantastic nanny—but I'm sure that's not your lifetime aspiration. Although I have to admit, selfishly, I wish you could care for Jerred and Ashley until they hit high school." He laughed.

He jabbed a log on the fire and it tumbled over, shooting sparks out from underneath. Jessica watched the sparks fly up the dark chimney, in such a hurry to escape only to be extinguished by the rain outside.

"It's just that I can't stand to see such a bright and capable young person spend her life caring for someone else's kids," he continued. "I know I might kick myself later, Jessie. I'm probably risking the best thing that's happened to this family in a long time, but you need to consider your future."

She didn't know what to say. His words warmed her, but how could she respond? He had no idea what had brought her on this mission. No idea his wife was really her mother.

"Have you considered college, Jessie? If finances are a problem, maybe we could work something out. Maybe you could live here, go to college, and still work part time for us. Our law firm has been known to give out scholarships occasionally."

It was a tempting offer, but she looked down and shook her head. She couldn't stand to continue this deception. He was so kind and caring. "I don't know. . . . It's so hard—"

He cut her off. "You know, Susan's life was hard, too, but she pulled herself up and made something out of it."

Jessica looked at him with curiosity. Maybe he could fill in some of the blanks about Susan after she gave her up. "Really? How's that?"

"For starters, Susan grew up in this crummy orphanage back East. You see, both her parents were killed when she was only six. She's had a very tragic life—I can hardly get her to talk about it. Then no one wanted to adopt her because she was too old. I think that's why she has such a hard time with this family thing, being a mother and all. That's why I try to give her lots of space. I figure in time she'll appreciate everything and come around. My point is this: Susan managed to pull herself up. She worked her way through business college and made a success of her life."

Jessica couldn't bear to look at him. This story was just too much. Orphanages, dead parents. . . . How could Susan lie to this kind, trusting man—her own husband? Jessica was ashamed of her mother.

David closed the glass doors on the fireplace and sat on the hearth before her. He looked into her eyes with sincere concern. "Jessie, you're a very special person. I've seen you with the kids. I just know you can make something truly great out of your life."

"Pretty cozy in here," said Susan sarcastically from the darkened kitchen.

David smiled and turned toward the kitchen. "Susan, you're home! I was just having a heart-to-heart with Jessie about her future. Come join us, will you? I know you'll agree, even though she's a super nanny, she really should consider college or something."

"Hmm?" Susan shook the droplets off her jacket and strode into the family room, viewing them suspiciously. "I don't know. . . ." She stood silently, arms folded in front. Her eyes narrowed as if she had caught them doing something wrong. First Jessica couldn't believe it. Then she felt cheap and almost guilty.

"Well, it's been a long day," said Jessica. She wanted to escape Susan's burning gaze. "I think I'll turn in. Good night." She hurried past Susan to her room. She sat on the bed and slowly grew more and more angry. Susan had no right to treat her like this.

Their voices traveled through the intercom, and Jessica

reached to flick it off, but instead her hand froze on the knob.

"Got your eye on the nanny, I see," said Susan in an ugly, accusatory tone.

"Susan, you're crazy. I was just trying to give her some fatherly advice."

"Sure, I'll bet you were. Don't think I haven't seen you look at her, David. And you're always telling me how *great* she is at everything. As if I should take lessons from *her*. Well, maybe I *should* take lessons from her, because it appears she knows how to operate. She's got you enchanted, David. She could probably just twist you around her little finger—"

Jessica snapped it off. Angry tears burned in her eyes. How could her own mother talk like that about her? She lay across the bed. Her last shred of hope was gone. Susan would never be a mother to her. She hated Susan and decided she was finished with this charade. She wouldn't stay another day. She had to get away. If she weren't so tired she would leave tonight.

A door slammed, and she recognized the sound of the Cherokee pulling out of the driveway. Poor David, he deserved better than Susan. But this problem wasn't Jessica's. Not anymore. Nothing she could do would change anything for them. Poor Jerred and Ashley, they deserved better, too. Suddenly Jessica grew indignant. What right had one selfish woman to lie and deceive, to ruin the lives of three innocent people? She paced her tiny room like a caged animal, three steps forward, three steps back, again and again. Finally she knew she would burst if she didn't, at least once, give Susan a piece of her mind. She marched down the hall toward Susan's room and knocked loudly on the door.

"What is it?" asked Susan in an irate voice. Jessica walked right in. Susan looked up from her lounge in surprise. A thick edition of *Vogue* slipped from her lap and flopped to the floor. Susan stood and glared fiercely. "Jessica, how dare you walk right into my room? Of course, it's probably not the first time is it?"

Jessica looked at her mother, standing there in the same blue satin robe, just like the first day she had met her. Yet even now, Jessica hardly knew her any better than then, and what she did know was disgusting. Susan's face, stripped of makeup, looked tight and drawn and older. Jessica walked over and sat on the unmade bed. Unmade, because Jessica'd had a busy day burying a puppy and tending to children.

"Susan, I've had it with you!" It was funny, she'd once imagined calling Susan 'mother' in private, but now she knew she never would.

"*You've* had it with *me?* Well, how do you think I feel? I go out one night and come home to catch you putting the move on my husband—"

"Give it a rest, Susan! Sure, David's a nice guy. It's just too bad you don't know how nice! I cannot believe what he puts up with. You're a mess, Susan! Frankly, I'll be surprised if your marriage lasts another week. You're the most selfish woman I've ever met, and I can't believe the lies you've told David. Honestly, Susan, I am embarrassed to think that you actually *are* my mother! I came here hoping I'd get to know my own flesh and blood. And I'm leaving wishing I'd never met you!" Susan's eyes widened and her face visibly paled. Jessica felt surprised that her words could have such impact on this seemingly coldhearted woman.

"Is this true?" boomed David from just outside the bedroom door. Jessica gasped and turned in horror. She thought he was gone. She'd never meant for him to hear all this.

"Is this true?" he repeated, stepping inside and closing the door behind him. "Are you really Jessica's mother?" He stared hard at Susan, waiting for an answer. But Susan was speechless.

"Never mind," he said. He looked from one to the other, studying their faces. He closed his eyes and shook his head. He looked sick, and Jessica felt like she might throw up.

"Of course it's true. I can see it now, clear as day." He ran his fingers through his hair and stared up at the ceiling. Jessica felt his pain. She ached with him. She felt as if this were all her fault.

"I'm—I'm sorry," Jessica blurted, heading for the door.

"Wait a minute, Jessie!" he ordered. "I want to hear the facts. Sit down." Jessica obeyed, and Susan collapsed onto her velvety lounge, hands shielding her face.

David paced back and forth, rubbing his forehead as if in deep concentration, probably the way he looked in the courtroom. Piece by piece, he painfully extracted the truth out of Susan. At first she tried to hide behind tears and tantrums. But finally she gave in, as if it was a relief to get everything out in the open, once and for all.

"I was just so ashamed of my past," continued Susan, tears streaming down her face. "I buried everything. I made up those stories because they were so pathetic. I'd even come to believe them. Until Jessica came along . . ."

Jessica wasn't sure if that was an accusation or not, but it seemed her role was over. Slipping out with her head down, she returned to her room and sprawled across the bed. Her head throbbed and she felt completely empty and numb, as lifeless as the little brown pup on the street today. She lay there for a long time, willing to cease to exist. At least nothingness would be painless.

For the first time, she replayed the series of events that had taken her down this crazy, crooked road. She considered her choices and where they had finally gotten her. And now this felt like the end of the road. There was no place else to go, no one to turn to.

"God, help me," she whispered desperately. Hopelessness and fear pressed in upon her. Maybe God didn't want to listen to her. After all, she hadn't tried to listen to Him. She stared up into the ceiling, holding her breath. Maybe God didn't really exist. Maybe this was the end of the road.

Then she saw it. She knew she did! It looked like it was printed right into the plaster, but later she knew it couldn't have been. But she saw it as plain as day. It was Mom's old cross-stitched sampler that hung above the fireplace back in Kansas. It had been there forever. And she knew they were the words of Jesus.

"Come to me, all you who are weary and burdened, and I will give you rest. Take my yoke upon you and learn from me, for I am gentle and humble in heart, and you will find rest for your souls. For my yoke is easy and my burden is light."

She stared at the words without blinking, not wanting them to disappear. Tears streamed down the sides of her cheeks and into her ears. Finally the words faded from the ceiling, but she realized she knew them by heart. She had always known them, only somewhere down the line she'd forgotten their truth.

"Jesus," she whispered out loud. "I am weary and burdened. I do come to you. Please show me what to do, and give me rest. . . ." She sighed, and a peace washed over her. She knew it was there because it was something she hadn't experienced for a long, long time. She wanted to freeze this moment in time and feel like this forever, but just on the edge of this peace was a pressing cry for help.

She knew her mother, just down the hall, was lying on the brink of disaster. She knew it wasn't her fault, but something in her had changed. Now she cared. Jessica found herself begging God to have mercy on Susan. And to her own amazement, Jessica experienced deep sympathy for this selfish woman so bent on destroying her own life. She prayed for a long time, sometimes wordlessly, sometimes incoherently. Eventually she fell asleep, still praying.

She awoke later, still peaceful and astonishingly refreshed for such a short period of sleep. She realized the intercom was off, and it was after three A.M. It was the time when Ashley usually cried out for her nightly feeding.

The nursery light glowed in Ashley's room, and Jessica peeked around the door. To her surprise, Susan sat in the rocker feeding her own baby for a change. Susan's face was blotchy and swollen, and another wave of pity came over Jessica.

"Come in," whispered Susan, looking up. Jessica stepped in hesitantly. She was unsure of what to expect after their earlier exchange of cruel and hateful words. She sat on the floor by the rocker, pulling her T-shirt over her knees like a tent.

"I'm sorry, Jessica. I really am. For all those things I said. I don't really know why I'm like this, but I'm sorry."

Jessica nodded. "I'm sorry, too. I said some pretty mean things also. I never meant for things to turn out this way. . . ."

"David's leaving tomorrow."

Jessica stared at Susan. "What do you mean?"

"He's taking the kids to B.C. to live with his folks. He's talking about a separation."

"Oh no, Susan! Is that what you want?"

"Well, no. . . . At least, I don't think so. I'm not sure what I want. I'm not sure what I'm capable of. One thing for certain, I know I'm a disaster as a mother."

Jessica said nothing. She wanted to comfort Susan but didn't know how. It was true, Susan had been pretty hopeless as a mother.

"Do you hate me, Jessica?"

"No, of course not. I guess I hated you for a moment last night. But not anymore. Mostly I'm sorry for you. You always seem so unhappy. But Susan, I think if you wanted it badly enough, you could work this out. I think you and David could patch things up."

"Really? Do you really think so?" she asked hopefully.

"Yeah, I do. Last night something weird happened to me. I prayed. I mean, I think I've always believed in God, even though I've made some pretty stupid mistakes lately. But last night I really prayed, and it was like God was in the room with me, right there listening and agreeing with me. You should try it sometime, Susan."

"Hmm . . ." Susan stood and laid the sleeping baby in the crib, then returned to the rocker. "Jessie, I really am proud of you. As your mother, I mean. I know it didn't have anything to do with me. Betty and Dan deserve all the credit—and of course you do, too. But I'm proud just the same."

Nothing Susan could've said would have meant more. Jessica reached up and grasped her mother's hand, and for that moment time became inconsequential. For that fleeting instant, right there in Ashley's nursery, Jessica became a small child, clinging to her mother. Susan released her hand, and the moment was over.

———

The next morning, David silently dashed about the house gathering stroller, high chair, and packing all sorts of things into the back of the Cherokee. Susan was nowhere in sight, and Jessica noticed the BMW was already gone.

"We're going to Grandpa and Grandma's, Jessie!" exclaimed Jerred, nearly tackling her. "You're coming too, right, Jessie?"

"No, I've gotta go home, Jerred."

"No way—Jessie!" He wrapped his arms around her leg. "You can't leave. Who'll take care of me an' Ashley? Dad? Jessie's coming too, isn't she?" David just shook his head sadly, and Jerred's grasp tightened.

The lump in her throat grew, and she kneeled down to look into Jerred's face. "Jerred, I'll be praying that God will take special good care of you. But you've got to understand, Jerred, right now I need to go home. I really need to see my family and my horse. Remember my horse, Jerred? He's missing me. He needs me." Jerred nodded solemnly, as if he could understand how a horse might need her. "Jerred, I'd love it if you could come visit me sometime on the farm."

His eyes grew wide. "Really, Jessie? You mean it? Could I ride your horse and play cowboys an' stuff?" She nodded with tears in her eyes.

"That'd be great, Jessie," said David. "We might just take you up on it."

She stood and looked at David. "I'm sorry about everything turning out this way—"

"Don't be sorry, Jessie. I think you came our way right in the nick of time. I knew things weren't right around here, but I was keeping my head in the sand, hoping everything would just work itself out. I see now it never would have. You can't build a marriage on lies. I'm not sure what's ahead, but we couldn't go on like that." He busied himself with the suitcases.

"But what about Susan, David?"

"She's gone." His hurt still showed in his voice.

"But what about your marriage?" She knew she should let it drop, but she cared too much not to ask.

"Don't worry, Jessie." He tried to smile and put a light tone in his voice. "I haven't completely given up on her yet. But the ball's in her court now. We'll just have to wait and see what she wants to do with it."

"Do you know where she went?" Jessica figured she might be able to stay with her for a few days before trying to get back to Kansas, maybe get to know her after all.

"I noticed our address book opened up to her old roommate's name. I expect she's gone there to lick her wounds for a while."

"Oh . . ." Jessica wondered what she should do.

"Do you need anything, Jessie? Do you have money for your airfare home?"

She looked down in embarrassment. "Well, actually, I never got paid for being your nanny. I mean, I know Susan's my mom and everything, and maybe I shouldn't—"

"You're kidding, Jessie! You were never paid? And you'd just let us take off without paying you? Don't you realize you've been worth a fortune these last few weeks? How did you expect to get back to Kansas? Or are you like Dorothy— were you just going click your heels together three times?"

She smiled. "That idea occurred to me once."

Jessica wrote Susan a long goodbye letter. She begged her to keep in touch. Jerred chattered all the way to the airport. At the ticket counter, David purchased Jessica's ticket and handed it to her along with a sealed envelope.

"Thanks for everything, Jessie," David said, clasping her hand warmly. "You were really a terrific nanny. If you ever need a recommendation . . . of course, I really hope you'll try to do something more with your life."

"Thank you, too, David. And thanks for being such a great dad to my brother and sister." She smiled down at Jerred and tousled his hair. Jerred's face looked confused.

"That's right, little man," said his dad. "Jessie's really your sister." Jerred grinned and hugged her again. "And Jessie," continued David, "when you decide to go to college, there're a few good ones right here in Seattle. You'd be more than welcome to stay with us. So stay in touch, okay?"

In no time, her plane was zipping straight across the sky and across the country. She marveled at how quickly she would be home, especially after what felt like years of running away. She opened the envelope David had given her and found five crisp one-hundred-dollar bills. She could use them to help pay back Dad and Todd.

Still, happy as she was to be going home, she was also filled with uncertainty. What would they say to her? Would they welcome her? Or treat her like a stranger? In her heart she felt sure they wanted her back, but part of her was still worried and anxious. She remembered about giving her cares to Jesus and finally relaxed. Besides, she knew she could always share Zephyr's stall; he'd be glad to see her.

She stepped from the jet's ramp down to the sun-baked tarmac of the Wichita airport feeling light-headed and dizzy.

She curbed the urge to bend over and kiss the Kansas turf. She was almost home! At one time Wichita's size would have overwhelmed and even terrified her, but now she felt confident as she caught the taxi to the bus station. On the bus to Poloma, she tried to corral her thoughts. She wanted to rehearse her apologies to her family, but instead she dozed off.

Finally, the bus pulled onto the road in front of the farm and stopped. She stepped off the bus and walked down the long driveway. She felt like this was a dream. She couldn't feel her feet touching the dusty gravel, and her eyes hungrily surveyed every dear and familiar detail of the old homestead. "There's no place like home," she repeated happily, just like Dorothy. Nearby, the big combine ran noisily. She loved that sound. And right behind followed the string of grain trucks catching the golden fountain of grain as it poured from the combine. They always reminded her of giant baby ducks trailing after their long-necked mother. This was a busy time, and she didn't want to distract them or interrupt work that would not wait. Maybe she could slip into the house unnoticed. She recognized Todd's lanky form sitting high up in the combine. That had been her job the past couple of years. He appeared to be looking her direction and suddenly the machine stopped.

He leaped down and yelped, racing toward her like a wild colt. She dropped her bag and cut through the stubble field. One by one, the other trucks halted and their drivers climbed out. She saw Danny, then Greg, and finally Dad made his way toward her, more slowly. Her heart beat fast, and suddenly she remembered their last encounter—that awful night almost two months ago when she'd been caught with Barry! She'd been so humiliated in front of her brothers, and Dad had been so angry.

Todd reached her first. His face was grinning as he grabbed her up and swung her about like a rag doll. Her other brothers joined the reunion, exchanging more hugs and smiles. She instantly forgot her misgivings about her brothers. Still Dad lingered a few feet back, wearing an expression she couldn't quite read. He scratched his whiskered chin and squinted into the late afternoon sun, still saying nothing. Everyone waited, expectantly.

Jessica looked at him then down at her feet. "Dad, I'm so sorry for everything. I know I've been an absolute fool and I don't even deserve your forgiveness. If you don't want me back, I'll understand—"

"That's enough now—you fellas get back to work," Dad ordered gruffly. Her brothers started moving away, going back to their trucks. "And as for you, young lady. You better get inside to your mother."

He took his hat by the brim and snapped it across his knee, sending dust and chaff flying, and looked her square in the eye. "And then I expect you right back out on this combine—pronto! You hear? We got work to do, Jessica Victoria!"

His weathered face wrinkled into that old familiar grin and she ran to him. He gave her a long, tight hug. Jessica knew she was home.

Teen Series From
Bethany House Publishers

—∞∞∞—

Early Teen Fiction (11–14)

HIGH HURDLES by Lauraine Snelling
Show jumper DJ Randall strives to defy the odds and achieve her dream of winning Olympic Gold.

SUMMERHILL SECRETS by Beverly Lewis
Fun-loving Merry Hanson encounters mystery and excitement in Pennsylvania's Amish country.

THE TIME NAVIGATORS by Gilbert Morris
Travel back in time with Danny and Dixie as they explore unforgettable moments in history.

Young Adult Fiction (12 and up)

CEDAR RIVER DAYDREAMS by Judy Baer
Experience the challenges and excitement of high school life with Lexi Leighton and her friends—over one million books sold!

GOLDEN FILLY SERIES by Lauraine Snelling
Readers are in for an exhilarating ride as Tricia Evanston races to become the first female jockey to win the sought-after Triple Crown.

JENNIE MCGRADY MYSTERIES by Patricia Rushford
A contemporary Nancy Drew, Jennie McGrady's sleuthing talents promise to keep readers on the edge of their seats.

LIVE! FROM BRENTWOOD HIGH by Judy Baer
When eight teenagers invade the newsroom, the result is an action-packed teen-run news show exploring the love, laughter, and tears of high school life.

THE SPECTRUM CHRONICLES by Thomas Locke
Adventure and romance await readers in this fantasy series set in another place and time.

SPRINGSONG BOOKS by various authors
Compelling love stories and contemporary themes promise to capture the hearts of readers.

WHITE DOVE ROMANCES by Yvonne Lehman
Romance, suspense, and fast-paced action for teens committed to finding pure love.

9606